Treachery and Truth

Treachery and Truth

A Story of Sinners, Servants, and Saints

by Katy Huth Jones

Pauline
BOOKS & MEDIA
Boston

Library of Congress Cataloging-in-Publication Data

Jones, Katy Huth.
  Treachery and truth : a story of sinners, servants, and saints / by Katy Huth Jones.
    pages cm
  Summary: "The story of St. Wenceslaus as told by his servant, Poidevin"--
  Provided by publisher.
  ISBN 978-0-8198-7535-8 (pbk.) -- ISBN 0-8198-7535-X (pbk.) 1. Wenceslas,
  Duke of Bohemia, approximately 907-929--Juvenile fiction. [1. Wenceslas, Duke
  of Bohemia, ca. 907-929--Fiction. 2. King, queens, rulers, etc.--Fiction. 3.
  Christian life--Fiction.] I. Title.
  PZ7.1.J7Tr 2016
  [Fic]--dc23
                                    2015027484

Cover photo by iStock.com/m-imagephotography

Photo of the bust of young Wenceslaus IV, King of Bohemia from the Treasury of Saint Vitus Cathedral in the Holy Cross Chapel at the Prague Castle by Packare, courtesy WikiMedia Commons, https://commons.wikimedia.org/wiki/File:Busta_Vaclav.jpg.

Photo of Saint Wenceslaus' sword from the Treasury of Saint Vitus Cathedral in the Holy Cross Chapel at the Prague Castle by Packare, courtesy WikiMedia Commons, http://commons.wikimedia.org/wiki/File:SvatovaclavskyMec.jpg.

Backcover image Mary Emmanuel Alves, FSP

Cover and book design by Mary Joseph Peterson, FSP

This is a novelized story including Saint Wenceslaus (Václav I, Duke of Bohemia). While Saint Wenceslaus is real, elements of this story—including some characters, conversations, the plot, and events—are fictional products of the author's imagination.

"P" and PAULINE are registered trademarks of the Daughters of Saint Paul.

Published by Pauline Books & Media, 50 Saint Paul's Avenue, Boston, MA 02130–3491

Printed in the U.S.A.

www.pauline.org

Pauline Books & Media is the publishing house of the Daughters of Saint Paul, an international congregation of women religious serving the Church with the communications media.

1 2 3 4 5 6 7 8 9   20 19 18 17 16

This book is dedicated to Pamela Sharp,
my longtime writing friend and fellow bibliophile,
without whom Poidevin's story
would never have been told.

Cast of Characters

Václav (VAHTS-lahv): Duke of the Přemysl dynasty, son of Dragomíra, brother to Boleslav and Přibislava

Poidevin (POI-duh-vin): A servant of Dragomíra and later Václav

Ludmila (LOOD-mil-ah): Grandmother of Václav, Boleslav, and Přibislava

Dragomíra (DRAH-goh-meer-ah): Mother of Václav, Boleslav, and Přibislava

Boleslav (BOH-luh-slahv): Younger brother of Václav, older brother of Přibislava

Přibislava (PRZHEE-bih-slahv-ah): Younger sister of Václav and Boleslav

Žibrid (ZHEE-brid): A *voyvode* loyal to Václav

Ana (AH-nuh): Daughter of Žibrid

Zbraslav (ZBRAH-slahv): Son of Václav and Ana

Žito (ZHEE-toh): Václav's trusted bodyguard

Father Pavel (PAH-vel): Catholic priest

Father Balád (BAH-lahd): Associate of Father Pavel

Bora (BOH-rah): A washerwoman who befriends Poidevin

Arnost (AR-nost): A shepherd living near Praha

Jan (YAHN): A blacksmith from a village on Bohemia's western border

Ladislav (LAH-dih-slahv): A *voyvode* loyal to Dragomíra

Tunna (TUH-nah): One of Dragomíra's henchmen

Gommon (GOH-mon): Another of Dragomíra's henchmen

Henry the Fowler: King of Saxony, a Germanic land on Bohemia's northwest border; a fowler traps and hunts birds

Arnulf (AR-noolf): Duke of Bavaria, a Germanic land on Bohemia's western border

Radslav (RAHD-slahv): Duke of Kourím (KOO-rheem)

Přemysl (PRZHE-mih-sil): First leader of the Čechs

Peoples, Places, and Things in the Tenth Century

Bavaria (buh-VAIR-ee-uh): A Germanic country bordering Bohemia on the west

Bohemia (boh-HĒ-mē-uh): A land of Eastern Europe now in the Czech Republic

Čech (CHEK): A tribe of people living in Bohemia

Drudge: An unskilled kitchen slave responsible for the lowliest tasks

Fortnight: Two weeks or fourteen days

Levý Hradec (LEH-vya HRAH-dets): Site of first church in Bohemia, about 10 kilometers or 6.2 miles from Praha

Magyars (MOD-yars): People from what is now Hungary

Midden (MID-in): Place where all the human filth and refuse of the castle was collected; someone was required to muck it out once a year

Moravia (moh-RAH-vee-ah): A Slavic country to the east of Bohemia

Praha (PRAH-hah): Capital of Bohemia/today's Czech Republic, known in English as Prague

Saxony (SAX-suh-nee): A Germanic country bordering Bohemia on the northwest

Scullion (SKULL-yuhn): A servant who scrubs floors or kitchen kettles

Tetín (TEH-teen): Castle where the Duchess Ludmila lived

Trencher bread: Bread used as a plate, common from the early Middle Ages

Vltava (VUHL-tah-vah): A river flowing through Praha/Prague. Known today by its German name, the Moldau.

Voyvode (VOY-vohd) : A warlord or chieftain of the Čechs, in later times a noble

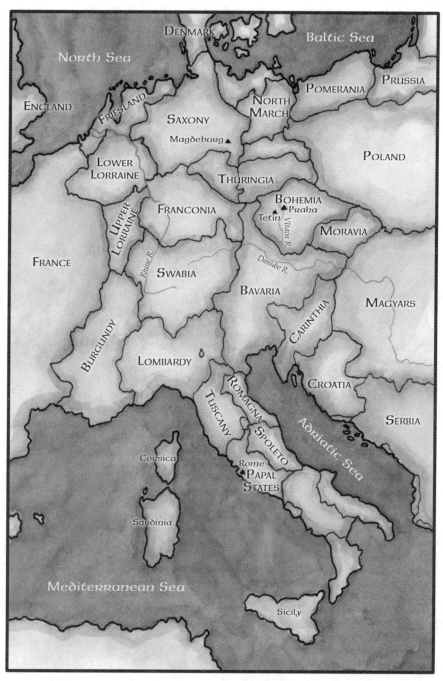

CENTRAL EUROPE IN THE 10ᵀᴴ CENTURY

Prologue

29th day of September
Feast of Michaelmas
Anno Domini 929

I, Poidevin, write this so that all may know the true story of
my master, the Duke of Bohemia, the most noble Václav. Though
our enemy is strong, the Most High is stronger still.
God, forgive me! I could not save him from his murderers. But
I hope I shall be granted enough time to write the truth, even as
my blessed master taught me.
Yet how can I write these words without baring my heart?
Even now the emotions of the past eight years fill my thoughts, as
if I were living them again.

Chapter 1

ARKNESS GRIPPED BOHEMIA, an evil born of fear:
Fear of the goddess Morana and her demand for
human sacrifice; fear of the nomadic Magyars who
had destroyed Moravia on our eastern border; and fear of the
mighty Germanic army to the west.

During those dark days, I bathed my mother's burning face
with my tears and listened to her incoherent mumbling until the
fever consumed her. For three days and nights I sat beside her,
until she followed my father in death. As soon as her body lay
cold in the ground, I was sold into bondage to pay my father's
debts.

Eight years ago . . . I was only twelve winters old and small
for my age. Nonetheless, a soldier shackled my right ankle and
joined me to a chain of other slaves. The rough metal scraped at
my skin with every step until I felt a warm trickle of blood.

I did not look at the other slaves or the soldiers. I concentrated on putting one bare foot in front of the other as the dirt
road carried me far from my village, the only home I'd ever
known. The other slaves never spoke to me. I suppose they were
as afraid as I was to draw the attention of our captors, especially
when we passed a sacred grove with an idol protected inside a
wooden shrine. As the smallest of the captives, I would be the
one to be sacrificed, had the guards felt the need to appease the
local god.

But on the third day of our journey, as we stopped for the night, I heard the oldest man among us say, "We will see Praha tomorrow."

Praha! My parents sometimes talked about the Duke of Bohemia who lived there. He had been killed in a recent battle with the Magyars, so now his wife, the duchess, ruled in his stead. *Why were we going to Praha?* I wondered. *What would we do there?*

The following day I laid aside my grief. While I still ached for my mother, I knew I could not bring her back, not with all the tears in Bohemia. I had to be ready to meet my fate. My heart filled with dread at my first sight of the fortress on a hill above the walled city of Praha. The wooden castle appeared massive enough to house all of Bohemia's gods.

I climbed the winding road up the hill with the other slaves. Our escort of soldiers whacked us with the shafts of their lances whenever we slowed down. As we reached the top, I stumbled, and one of the soldiers growled and jerked me to my feet. A vile stench reached my nostrils, and I glanced up to see rotting heads and skulls on pikes along the castle wall. My empty stomach heaved.

What demons lived here? Was I purchased to be sacrificed to one of the gods?

We entered the castle yard, and the soldiers lined us up for inspection. A nobleman looked each of us over, as if we were horses for sale.

Stables, he said, pointing to an older man. Laundry. He indicated a young woman. Kitchen, to a boy not much older than I.

The nobleman grabbed my chin with one gloved hand and pushed back my shaggy hair with the other. He turned my head first one way and then the other. Then he forced open my mouth and checked my teeth. "This one," he said, "is for the duchess."

My heart skipped a beat, for I was certain the duchess would use me for a sacrifice. But a woman took me to a room where I was given a plain but nearly new tunic made of soft fabric, a rag, and a small basin of water.

"Wash," the woman commanded. "Then dress and report to the steward in the hall."

I did so, trembling as I entered the hall. The high ceiling and the lack of windows made the room seem like a cavern. Torches burned in brackets set in the walls. Their flickering light made every shadow dance.

Another man, wearing a fine embroidered tunic, stepped toward me from the shadows. "Boy," he said, straightening my own shorter tunic. "I will present you to the duchess. You must bow to her, not speak unless you are spoken to, and do whatever she bids you."

"Yes, sir." My whisper was barely audible. My legs felt like water. I followed the steward to the other end of the hall where an elegant woman sat at table with several richly attired noblemen. I stopped when the steward did and tried not to stare at the men and woman as they conversed. I hoped the fact that they'd just given me a new tunic meant that they would not offer me as a sacrifice. Unless they wanted their sacrifices clean and well fed first. . . .

"Your Highness," said the steward with a bow. He slapped my shoulder and I fell to my knees on the rush-covered flagstones. "I bring you a new servant, just arrived."

The steward did not move, and neither did I, so I could not see the duchess's face.

"A new servant? What was wrong with the old one?" Her voice was husky and conveyed disdain. The noblemen chuckled at her words.

I heard the rustle of her skirts as she stood and walked around the table. Into my field of vision came a length of heavy fabric with the toes of two slippers just visible at the hem.

"Stand up, boy, and let me look at you."

I swallowed and struggled to my feet, though I would not raise my head. The duchess jerked my head up by a hank of hair. I gasped as she gazed into my eyes. Hers were black and cold, serpent's eyes.

"He's small," she said to the steward. "Will he work or will he end up like that insolent wretch you brought me last time?"

"Your Highness, the boy will grow. And upon my life he will work for you." The steward bowed even lower.

The duchess turned away. "Take him to my rooms and have him clean them."

The steward led me up a narrow staircase to the duchess's spacious rooms. The disorder I found there seemed at odds with her personal appearance. Someone had scattered dozens of embroidered cushions. Goblets and platters littered the floor, along with spilled wine and food.

"What happened to the last servant?" I managed to ask.

The steward threw a menacing look at me. "His head greeted you at the gate." He indicated the mess. "Get to work."

Thus began my service to the widowed Duchess Dragomíra. From the other servants I discovered that she was not Čech, but the daughter of a chieftain from the north. She was cruel, they said, like her father. Having seen the grisly row of heads outside, I had no trouble believing it.

Though the servants whispered to me about the duchess, always glancing over their shoulders before doing so, they also spoke of Prince Václav.

"He is coming back to Praha," a scullion said about a month later as we scrubbed the floor of the great hall. We were to make it ready for the Feast of Midsummer.

"Who is *he*?" I asked.

The boy scowled as if only I could be so dense. "*He* is the duke's heir, once he comes of age." Then he leaned closer. "Prince Václav scorns the gods of Bohemia and makes no sacrifices of blood."

"What? Does he not fear their wrath?" I stopped scrubbing for a moment, shocked at the boldness of this prince.

The boy shrugged and wrung out his rag. "They say he worships only one high God, but the duchess has outlawed his religion." He lowered his voice. "Have you seen the heads?"

I nodded, swallowing. They haunted my dreams.

"They were followers of Václav's God."

I shuddered and applied myself to scrubbing the floor.

Chapter 2

T THE FEAST that evening, I stood before the head table pouring wine for my lady Dragomíra; her younger son, Boleslav; and her only daughter, Přibislava, when the door to the great hall flew open with a crash. All sounds of revelry faded away. The song the bard plucked from the harp he held on his lap ceased, though a faint echo of music hung in the air as a young man strode in.

"Prince Václav," I heard someone mutter.

I stared at the prince as he approached the head table. He wore a black woolen robe under a coarse mantle, and his dark hair was cut short. His face was beardless, his build slender and youthful. Yet he was, I had to admit, more of a commanding presence than I had imagined.

Václav stopped at the table and bowed to the Duchess Dragomíra.

"Greetings, Mother, and greetings to you, my brother and my sister."

Prince Boleslav was my age, about twelve years, but looked older because he had been well fed all his life. He did not smile at his elder brother, though young Přibislava did.

"We are glad you have come to our feast, Václav," said Dragomíra.

"I don't care to feast, Mother," Václav said. "I've just learned of your new laws."

"And are you offended by laws set down by the rightful regent of Bohemia?" Boleslav asked, crossing his arms.

"You know that I am." Václav turned back to their mother. "Why would you forbid the priests, on pain of death, to teach children Latin and music? There are no better teachers in all Bohemia."

"They teach what is not prudent for children to learn," Dragomíra said through clenched teeth.

"They teach truth." Václav laid both hands on the trestle table. I noticed he wore no jewels, unlike his brother. "Would you kill a man for teaching truth?"

"What you call 'truth' is an outrage to the ancient gods of Bohemia," Boleslav sneered.

"Truth is truth for all," said Václav. "I will not allow these persecutions to continue."

"You will obey me," Dragomíra said with growing anger, "and stay well away from those accursed priests. Would that I had never allowed you to live with your grandmother! She filled your head with empty words."

Václav leaned forward. His eyes blazed with fervor. "My grandmother opened my eyes to the truth, the Gospel of our blessed Christ that you so stubbornly resist. For that I shall always be grateful. She is a devout and kind woman, and she still wields much influence from the days of her husband's reign. Or have you forgotten that my grandfather also followed the Most High God, as did my father?"

Dragomíra stared coldly at Václav.

"And as you once claimed to do," he added.

The duchess did not answer. Přibislava turned her head away as if she were ashamed.

"You *will* change the decree, Mother."

Dragomíra stood up and smacked her hand on the table. "*You* will obey me, Václav, or I'll have your head!"

The prince turned on his heel and left the hall. A few of the chieftains and courtiers followed him out.

As I scrambled down the stone steps to the kitchen to fetch my lady a fresh piece of trencher bread, I realized that this son of hers was not at all what I expected. He was not much older than I was, no more than fourteen, yet he had confidence and presence of mind that I had never seen in one of his years.

Later that evening while serving my lady in her private quarters, she accepted Boleslav and five local *voyvodes*, or warlords, into the sitting room where she received visitors. A cool breeze blew through the open window. Flickering candlelight reflected in the gold threads of the stag tapestry on the wall. As soon as the men sat down on wooden stools, Dragomíra glanced my way.

"That is all," she said, dismissing me.

I turned to go as they began speaking in hushed voices. Before I reached the door, I remembered a pile of rags that needed washing, so I went into the next room to get them.

"It is imperative that young Václav not come to power at this time," said a deep voice.

I inched closer to the doorway to hear what was said.

"With the dowager Duchess Ludmila's influence, he would put us under Germanic power," said another.

"My loyal *voyvodes*," Dragomíra said, "if Ludmila's influence over Václav were to end, it would solve many problems. And without his grandmother, my eldest son will not have the backing he needs to press his claim to the throne." I stifled a gasp when I realized what they were plotting. "I plan to *encourage* our pious prince to pursue a monastic life, one that better suits his religious convictions."

There was low laughter, and they began to discuss how to do away with Ludmila, the old duchess who used to bring food and firewood to our village every winter. "She is so kind, Poidevin," Mama often said to me. "Though she has wealth and power, still she cares for the least of us poor villagers."

I became frightened, not only for Duchess Ludmila, but for my life as well. What if the conspirators found out I was listening?

Dropping the soiled rags, I climbed out to the balcony and down the thick vines that clung to the wall. Once in the courtyard, I pondered what to do. Undoubtedly I should warn Prince Václav that his grandmother was in danger, but I had no idea where to find him or how to tell him. The only person I knew I could trust not to behead me for my knowledge was the old washerwoman, Bora, who had been kind to me from the day I met her. She remained loyal to the memory of the recently departed duke and his parents, and she was the only person in Praha who knew my name or even cared that I had one.

Holding my head high, I strode past the guards at the open castle gate. I felt their stares at my back, but they did not question me. As soon as I saw the thatched roof of Bora's wooden hut just outside the castle wall, I ran toward it.

"Bora," I called as loudly as I dared when I reached the doorway of the hut. She lived with her husband, who had a wasting disease, caring for him as she had their nine babes. The stench of his illness in my nostrils assaulted me, though Bora never seemed to notice.

"What is it, Poidevin?"

I took a moment to gulp a deep breath from the outside air and then leaned toward her. "The old duke's wife, Ludmila, is in terrible danger," I whispered.

"Danger?" She caught me by the arms. "What do you mean? How do you know?"

"I heard the duchess speaking with some men just now. They were planning to kill her!"

"But why?" Bora said. "Why would they want to kill a good woman, an old woman?"

"Something about Prince Václav. I don't understand it, but we've got to warn him, and I don't know how."

Bora frowned. "The prince will see me," she said, patting my hand.

Now I was puzzled. "Do you know him, then?"

Bora stared at me, her tired eyes reflecting wariness. But then she smiled, and her eyes glowed with something I'd never seen before. Was it peace?

"Yes, Poidevin, I do know Prince Václav, because he is my brother in the faith."

I gaped at her. Before speaking I made sure no one stood near the doorway, but still I whispered, "You don't mean you are a follower of his God?"

She nodded. "Yes, I am a Christian too."

I swallowed as I realized the great trust Bora had just shown to me. After all, I served Duchess Dragomíra, who would behead both of us—Bora for being a Christian, and me for not reporting what I knew. "I will never tell my mistress."

Bora patted my hand again. "I know you won't, Poidevin." She smiled again, that peaceful, glowing smile. "I will speak to the prince. Now don't worry."

I ran back to the great hall, trying very much not to worry. I now knew that my mistress was as cruel and ruthless as I'd heard she was. If she would plot the death of an old woman, her own mother-in-law, what could she do to me?

Chapter 3

*T*HE NEXT FEW days I feared my mistress would discover I had told Bora of her intention to murder the old duchess. I imagined myself imprisoned—or worse, beheaded —for what I'd done. It was a wonder she did not suspect something from my actions. While serving her at table I dropped a platter of food and spilled wine when I refilled her goblet. Boleslav kicked me, and I did receive a sound thrashing from the steward. But I counted myself fortunate that it ended there.

I began to pay more attention to the conversations between the duchess and her *voyvodes*, and to the servants as they worked inside the castle and also in the yard. What I heard opened my eyes to a larger world than I had ever known in the small village I'd lived in before.

I saw for myself the hierarchy of power and began to understand the way things were ordered. The Duchess Dragomíra ruled all of Bohemia, though it was apparently smaller and less important than other nations. She and the *voyvodes* lived in luxury from the wealth of Bohemia: its land, the crops, the animals, and the labor of the farmers, villagers, and, of course, slaves.

I had been simple, indeed, to think that the land my father farmed and the cottage my mother tended had been truly ours. I had been in bondage my entire life without realizing it. I also began to understand that being a personal servant to the duchess of Bohemia, while constantly requiring my attention and effort, was a much better form of bondage than those my age who toiled in the fields, cleaned out stables, or worse, the castle middens.

I found myself always surrounded by gossip and chatter. To my surprise, none of it was about the old Dowager Duchess Ludmila. Consequently, I began to think that the plans to kill her had been my imagination, and I lost my fear of being discovered. About a fortnight later, however, I was suddenly and forcibly reminded what kind of mistress I served.

Dragomíra sat at the head table for the evening meal with her three children. As time passed, Boleslav grew more and more sullen. I wondered if he intended to provoke a fight. Václav, on the other hand, ate little, and conversed quietly with his sister, Přibislava. Their table was an island of tension and hostility surrounded by laughter and clanking goblets.

Just as I served my mistress from a plate of meats, a messenger ran into the room and fell to the rush-covered floor. He flushed, gasping for air.

"My lady," he began, shuddering. The man desperately tried to catch his breath.

The duchess leaned forward. "Yes, what is it?"

The messenger pulled off his cap, wiped the sweat from his brow.

Dragomíra stood up. "Out with it!"

"I've come from Castle Tetín, my lady," the man said, rising to his knees. "Duchess Ludmila has been murdered."

I held my breath. For a heartbeat the room became silent. Then Prince Václav slowly stood and whispered, "No."

The duchess frowned, but her eyes glittered with satisfaction. Boleslav seemed to have difficulty concealing a smirk.

"She was strangled," the messenger said, near tears. "She was praying in her private chapel, and someone strangled her with her veil."

As the duchess smoothed her own veil, I noticed she pushed it away from her throat. Had she chosen the time and place of her mother-in-law's death? Was it mere chance that Ludmila had been praying to the Christian God when she died, or was it intended to show Dragomíra's contempt for the new religion?

Přibislava covered her face with her hands and began to weep. Václav placed a hand on her shoulder as he spoke to the messenger. "Did anyone see the murderer?"

"Yes, Your Grace." The man twisted his cap. "A servant saw two men running from the chapel, but could not identify them. The captain of the guard is questioning others who might have seen them."

The prince turned to his mother. "I shall leave for Tetín at once."

"Of course, Václav. I know how close you were to your grandmother." She folded her hands and forced her mouth into that same sorrowful pose. "I grieve with you, my son."

Surprised at her words, I looked more closely at Dragomíra's face. I knew grief, intimately, but I saw none in the duchess. What I did see was false.

Prince Václav said no more. He kissed his sister on the cheek and went out with the distraught messenger. As soon as they left the room, I headed to the kitchen to fetch a fresh wineskin. I heard snatches of conversation from others in the hall as they discussed the murder of the old Duchess Ludmila.

At the door I glanced back at the head table. Boleslav smiled at his mother, and Dragomíra dropped her pretense of sorrow by finishing the contents of her goblet. Serpents! Both of them! But I forced all emotion from my thoughts before I served them. I didn't dare reveal my true feelings, or I would risk ending up as dead as Duchess Ludmila.

All that night I could not sleep. I tossed and turned on my bed of straw on the floor of the great hall. If I had been more bold, would the old duchess still be alive? Perhaps I should have gone to Prince Václav himself, but he might not have believed me. Besides, how would I have approached him? I was just a servant, and a servant was not supposed to speak first to anyone who was not also a servant, especially not a prince. Yet I could not shake the feeling that Duchess Ludmila's death was at least partially my fault.

Before the sun rose, I hurried down to Bora's hut. As I knew she would be, she was already up cooking for her husband.

"Bora," I whispered from the open doorway.

She whirled and saw me, then hung the ladle over the iron pot. "Oh, Poidevin." She sighed.

"Then you know?" I asked.

"Yes." Her eyes filled with tears. Dark circles rimmed her eyes, as if she had not slept all night, either.

"Did you warn the prince?" I whispered.

"Yes." She frowned. "I spoke with him myself, and he said he could not believe that his mother would conspire to do such a thing."

"He didn't believe you?"

Crack! At a sudden, sharp pain across my shoulders, I spun around. A guard on his way in from the night watch had whacked me with his lance.

"Stop gossiping, boy, and get to work."

I scampered away before the guard could take aim again.

The evening following Prince Václav's departure, two new faces appeared at table with my mistress. As soon as I saw the men, the hairs on the back of my neck prickled in alarm. Their coarse manners were at odds with their noble dress. I did not understand why the duchess would desire to be in the same room with them, much less invite them to eat at her table.

Boleslav laughed when one of them, named Gommon, cuffed me so hard that I tripped over one of the hounds lying on the straw. As I shook my head to clear it, I staggered to my feet. What had I done to merit that blow?

"Your slaves are quite resilient," said Tunna, the other visitor.

"Peace, Gommon, and you, Tunna," Dragomíra said with a frown. "Do not let your rise to favor go to your heads if you wish to keep them attached to your necks."

After that I stayed out of their way as much as possible. It was not until Prince Václav returned from Castle Tetín, however, that I discovered why the two men had "risen to favor."

I was cleaning up after another one of my lady's private meals in her room when Prince Václav came to see the duchess. He was still wearing his travel cloak.

"Tunna and Gommon were your agents," Václav said after the barest of greetings. "I have eyewitnesses who say they entered the chapel shortly before my grandmother went there to pray, and that two men were seen running from the chapel some time later."

"Václav," Dragomíra struggled to hold her anger in check, "I have known Tunna and Gommon for many years. They would have no reason to commit such a vile act."

"No?" said Václav. "Then why were they given part of the castle's treasure? Why was the treasure divided at all? Could you not have left it to the people of Tetín, the loyal subjects of my grandparents?"

Dragomíra shrugged. "I am the regent of all of Bohemia, Václav. I bestow the riches of this kingdom where they are most needed."

The prince clenched his fists. When he spoke again, the tone of his voice made me cringe.

"Mother, you have gone too far. The blood of my grandmother joins the heads of all the other murdered innocents crying out for justice. When I am Duke of Bohemia, goodness and the rule of law will prevail. May God have mercy on your soul."

He turned and strode down the hall. I trembled to think that the conflict between them could only grow. What would be the end of it?

Chapter 4

WOKE IN THE darkest part of the night, when all in the castle slept except a handful of guards. A kitchen drudge had pushed me off the straw, and I became so restless on the hard stone that I went out in the empty halls and wandered.

My wandering was without purpose. I suppose I hoped it might purge the guilt I felt about Duchess Ludmila's death to pad barefooted along the cold flagstones. I shivered in my tunic in the unseasonably cool summer night. Before I realized it, I had come to the tower where Václav had his rooms. A faint light shone through the slit under the heavy wooden door. I pressed my ear to the door and heard muffled voices.

To this day I do not know what possessed me to open that door. Perhaps it was the will of Václav's God. Nevertheless, I opened it slowly, carefully, and peered around it to see the prince sitting at a trestle table, dressed like the two black-robed priests who sat across from him. By the light of a single candle they pored over scrolls and books, speaking in earnest. They did not seem to notice me.

Had I closed the door and gone on my way, Václav would never have known I was there. But I lingered, curious, straining to hear what these three were discussing in the small hours of the night. From beside the door a heavy hand grabbed my arm and yanked me into the room, pushing me down to the straw-covered floor.

"What are you doing *here*?" said a harsh voice. When I looked up, I met the angry stare of a guard wearing leathers and a fur-lined cap, his other hand poised over the knife in his belt.

Before I could speak, Václav stood up and held out his hand to stay the guard.

"Peace, Žito," he said.

"You are too trusting, my lord," Žito said, still glaring at me. "This one is Dragomíra's own servant boy. He is a spy."

Though Žito had let go of my arm at Václav's word, I stayed on my knees, staring at the prince.

Václav walked toward me, his woolen robe swirling at his feet. I began to tremble, and wished I had never, never opened that door.

"My lord," I said, my voice shaking, "have mercy on me." I held up my hands to ward off the blow that was sure to fall.

He stopped and looked down at me. His gray eyes were kind. "You know who I am, then?" he asked.

"Yes, my lord." I sucked in a deep breath. "You are Prince Václav."

"But I do not know you. Tell me your name, Son."

He called me "son," as if he were much more than just a couple of years older than I.

"Poidevin, my lord." I swallowed the fear in my throat.

"Poidevin," Václav said, as if my name were important to him. "And how old are you?"

"I have twelve winters." I held up my head so he would not think me a foolish child.

"You serve my mother, the Duchess Dragomíra?"

"Yes, my lord," I said.

"Where is your family, Poidevin?" The words were spoken in such a kind voice that I wondered if Václav already knew what had happened to them.

"My parents are dead, my lord. I was sold into service here to pay my father's debts."

Václav turned away for a moment. When he looked back at me, his eyes were shining. It could not have been tears; not for a slave.

He cleared his throat before he spoke again. "Bora did not tell me anything about you, other than she is very fond of you and trusts you completely."

The prince's words startled me, for I did not think Bora would tell him who had overheard the plot against his grandmother. But I supposed Bora didn't have to tell him; Prince Václav could easily have deduced it was me.

Then all kinds of emotions rose within me. Chief among them was anger that Václav would not believe that his mother was capable of murder. But I swallowed my anger and did not say a word.

Václav regarded me with those clear gray eyes, kindly but firmly. "In light of your proven trustworthiness, I am wondering why you were listening at the door just now." He folded his hands and waited for my answer.

I had no good answer. My voice trembled when I spoke. "I was just wandering the halls, my lord, thinking. I didn't realize where I was until I saw the light under your door. When I came closer I heard quiet voices and wondered who was awake so late." I dropped my gaze. "I am sorry for intruding, my lord."

The prince remained silent until I looked up again. Then he smiled. "Don't you want to know what we are doing in the dark of the night?"

I blinked in surprise. "Y-yes, my lord," I answered truthfully.

Václav gestured to the table. "Father Pavel, Father Balád, and I were having a discussion on the subject of forgiveness."

"Forgiveness, my lord?"

He nodded. "It means to pardon, to show mercy." He paused. "Not to hold something against one who has wronged you."

I glanced at the scrolls on the table and wondered what they had to do with a discussion on forgiveness. I squinted at the open one nearest to me and puzzled at the black marks walking across like tiny footprints.

"Do you know how to read, Poidevin?"

The question took me by surprise. "No, my lord."

Václav smiled. "Would you like to learn?"

"My lord!" Žito cried. "What if the duchess has sent this boy to entrap you?" The priests added their opinions in a babble of voices.

The prince held up his hands. "Did not our blessed Master himself say, 'Let the children come unto me'?"

The priests said no more, but the burly Žito crossed his arms, clearly upset. Václav again turned his attention to me.

"What do you say, Poidevin? Would you like to learn to read?"

I flinched as if he'd struck me. A servant learn to read? What would the duchess say? I imagined she would put me to death for standing in the same room with these two priests, even more so if I returned to learn from them night after night.

But my life was worth nothing to her anyway. I could be killed at any time, even on a whim, even if I did nothing wrong. Was this risk so much greater than my present life? Learning could make my life more bearable for as long as it lasted.

I nodded my head, which started my tongue in motion again. "I would like to very much, but I don't wish to place you in danger from my mistress."

Václav placed his hands on my shoulders. His touch was warm, a comfort to me.

"Do not fear for my sake, Poidevin. I am not afraid of your mistress. My Master is greater than any evil a man or woman can do."

A chill ran down my spine at his words. Who was his master?

"We study here in this room every night at this time. Come tomorrow, and I will begin to teach you to read."

I glanced at the priests and boldly asked, "In Slavonic? Or in Latin?"

Václav laughed. "Both," he said, gesturing to the scrolls and books.

I nodded and stood. But before I could thank him, Václav's face grew solemn.

Something about the prince made me instinctively trust him and I spoke up, which I had never dared do with the duchess. "What is it, my lord?" Was he thinking about his grandmother?

Václav indicated the two priests. "Father Pavel and Father Balád come to me willingly, even though they know they will be killed if they are discovered here. It is vitally important, Poidevin, that you not let knowledge of their presence in the castle slip out in an unguarded moment."

My throat had gone suddenly dry, and I swallowed. "Of course, my lord. I would never wish for them to be in danger." I bowed to the prince. "I shall prove my trustworthiness to you."

Now Václav smiled again. "I'm sure you will, Poidevin."

Although I was reluctant to leave, I decided I had better get back to the servants' place on the floor of the great hall. I made another bow. "Thank you, my lord."

I slipped out the door and ran back to the hall as fast as I could. Even lying on the straw with only a thin blanket to cover me, I was no longer cold, for the knowledge that the prince trusted me and was going to teach me how to read kept me warm all night.

Chapter 5

*A*LL THAT FALL and winter I led a double life. By day I served Duchess Dragomíra, throwing myself wholeheartedly into every task to offset my nagging fear that she would somehow discover I was learning how to read and who was teaching me. I earned fewer and fewer stripes, but I also became more observant, more perceptive. The court at Praha was divided: about half were pagan, loyal to Dragomíra's policies to suppress by all means the followers of Václav's God and their supposed Germanic influence; the others, less vocal, were loyal to Bohemia, but had no wish to see innocent people persecuted. Apparently many of them had worshiped the Christian God during the reigns of Václav's father and grandfather. They seemed to dislike Dragomíra personally, but feared to say anything against her. Perhaps they were biding their time until Prince Václav could take over as duke.

By night I became Václav's student, but in more than just Latin and Slavonic. His two priests, Pavel and Balád, had been disciples of Methodius, who many years ago had come bringing the Christian religion to Bohemia for the first time. I'd grown up with many gods and a healthy fear of them, so this concept of only one high God was not easy to grasp. But for now, Václav was content that I learn to trust him and to read the letters for myself.

At first I found it difficult to function on such little rest. My zeal during the first two or three days gave way to such exhaustion that I found myself falling asleep in very inconvenient places—behind Dragomíra's chair or under the cook's feet in the kitchen. But bruises and the threat of more helped keep me awake when necessary until my body adjusted to having just three or four hours of sleep each night. Besides, Prince Václav insisted that each seventh night, the night before his weekly holy day, be spent in prayer. As he and the priests said their silent prayers, kneeling with their heads bowed and their eyes closed, I soon learned how to doze for most of the night while on my knees. That helped me make it through the rest of the week.

Žito, the prince's bodyguard, gradually came to trust me, too. After all, what had I to gain by telling the duchess that I studied Latin and Slavonic with her son every night? Žito must have known that I would suffer the same punishment as anyone else who consorted with the outlawed priests. Death.

I often wondered myself why I risked everything to go. Sometimes it seemed Václav had cast a spell on me, so strong was my devotion to him. But eventually I decided it was only his kindness, his genuine concern in a castle full of plotting, violent people that drew me to him. Where Bora the washerwoman was like a mother to me, Prince Václav became a father, the one who guided me and prepared me for the future, whatever it held.

Early that spring, not long after the first thaw, Dragomíra received a message from Arnulf, the Duke of Bavaria, to the south and west of us. I was serving her while she was in conference with her loyal *voyvodes* and courtiers.

"How dare he!" She threw the scroll to the table.

The *voyvodes* were accustomed to waiting patiently for an explanation to the duchess's outbursts. They had learned it would come, eventually.

Dragomíra tapped her fingers on the table next to her goblet of wine. Her face grew red with anger.

"The Bavarians have spoken," she said. "They demand our allegiance. They demand we pay an annual tribute to them as our rightful overlord, or they threaten to destroy us."

The *voyvodes* murmured and shook their heads.

"What will your answer be, Your Highness?" asked Ladislav, the eldest among them.

Dragomíra smiled. "What do you think? Has Bohemia become soft since the duke's death? Has my husband's army grown weak since he defeated the Magyars last spring? The army that vanquished the Magyars can most certainly crush a few Bavarians!"

Shoving back their chairs, the *voyvodes* lifted their goblets in salute.

"To Bohemia!"

"We will fight to the death—their death!"

"The Bavarians are nothing!"

With much clanking and clashing of goblets, as well as the spilled wine that I had to clean up later, the *voyvodes* agreed that messengers should be sent throughout Bohemia to call the fighting men to Praha. Within ten days an army would be sent to meet the Bavarian forces under Duke Arnulf, before he could advance across the border.

That afternoon I watched, along with most everyone else, as the soldiers in the castle drilled under Prince Václav, whom Dragomíra had appointed battle commander. I sighed, wishing I could be out there with them, swinging a sword and hearing it clash against a shield. I was thirteen then, growing taller and stronger. Would I ever have the chance? Was it ever possible for a slave to become a soldier?

I straightened with pride to see the prince astride his black horse. Václav was clad in chain mail and conical helm, and he held a lance with a pennon of red and white, the royal colors. It was difficult for me to reconcile this commander with the same young man who spoke so earnestly of peace among men and loving his enemies.

Had Dragomíra and Boleslav any idea that he daily prayed for them? That he honestly did not hate them, even though he believed them responsible for the death of his beloved grandmother? I did not think so.

Could I ever pray for my enemies? I couldn't imagine it.

A few days later the castle swelled to bursting with soldiers called from every village, and the surrounding countryside had filled with tents and camps. Václav gave the order to depart for the Bavarian border. I watched from the wall, crushed between women and servants. I waved as the army streamed away, screaming myself hoarse to be heard over the crowd. Prince Václav rode at the head of that legion. He appeared confident—trusting, as he told me the night before, that his God would grant him victory.

"But how do you know?" I had asked him. I wasn't sure I believed anyone could be so certain.

He had placed his hands on my shoulders and snared me with his eyes. "I have faith, Poidevin," he said. "I know my Master has a work for me to do, and this is only the beginning. He has never failed me, and he never will."

I nodded, though I still did not understand.

And though I secretly feared war and bloodshed and the pain of death, I also fervently wished I could ride beside Václav at the head of that vast, fierce army.

Chapter 6

FOR MANY DAYS the castle was quiet. We servants went about our work, but with an undercurrent of tension. Everyone had been so confident. But no one really knew who would ride back to the castle gates. Would it be Prince Václav—or Duke Arnulf?

I found that I greatly missed my late night sessions with Václav and the priests. For, of course, while he and Žito were gone from the castle, Father Pavel and Father Balád could not risk sneaking in. Their connection with sympathetic nobles or night guards was gone.

I had thought I might be able to catch up on some sleep during those days, but out of habit I awakened each night. Usually I tossed and turned in place, but one night I crept up the stairs to the tower where Václav's chapel stood empty. The candles were unlit, and the faint light from the waning moon barely outlined the shadowy form of the altar rail.

Kneeling, I folded my hands as I had seen Václav do, bowed my head, and closed my eyes.

I wanted to say something, but I wasn't sure what. The gods I knew of were wrathful and bloodthirsty. They punished those who did not sacrifice to them. I had learned what little I knew from my mother and from a pagan priest of the old religion who lived in the forest near my home. He had told me about the annual winter sacrifice to the forest god.

"The sacrifice," he had said, "has to be a boy, about your size." His stare penetrated me, as if he were baring my soul.

"A b-boy?" I had stammered.

"Yes." His grin revealed rotten teeth. "If your mother dies this winter, then maybe it will be you!"

I ran all the way home to my frail mother. That night was the first time our cottage had not seemed safe.

The following spring my mother did die. A year had passed since then.

Why was I remembering this? All I had intended was to ask Václav's God to protect the prince.

"God of Václav," I whispered, swallowing. Would he punish me if I said the wrong thing? "I am Poidevin, a lowly slave. I do not know you, but I know Prince Václav, and that he is just and good. Would you please watch over him and protect him from his enemies?"

I was very, very careful not to say anything evil against the Bavarians, since Václav had told me many times how his God wanted him to love even his enemies. Though I didn't expect an answer, I waited for a few minutes. All was quiet; maybe I was safe. At least fire had not come down from the sky to devour me. Sighing, I hurried back to bed.

The longest fortnight of my life dragged on between the time of my prayer and the arrival of a messenger at the castle. He proclaimed that Prince Václav's army had successfully repelled the invading Bavarians.

"So soon?" Duchess Dragomíra wondered aloud. She looked at Boleslav beside her, who had not gone with the army. Did Dragomíra think he was yet too young to fight? He and I were the same age, and I would have gladly fought at Prince Václav's side.

Boleslav shrugged. "Perhaps the Bavarians didn't want to fight after all."

I had to bite my tongue to keep from saying something to Boleslav. Did he hate his brother so much that he would make his great accomplishment look like nothing?

"Well," said Dragomíra, rising, "we must prepare a banquet for the returning victors." Her voice was cheerful, though I could see annoyance in the tightness of her mouth.

"All, my lady?" I asked before I could control my tongue. My shoulders hunched in anticipation of her reaction.

Instead of turning on me, the Duchess actually laughed. "No, boy. Our kitchen cannot feed an entire army in this one room. But we will honor the army's commander and his battle chiefs with a feast. The soldiers will be fed, never fear."

I wondered what kept her from striking me for my impertinence. But I felt relief, nonetheless.

Late the following afternoon, a lookout spotted the approaching army, and everyone in the castle swarmed the battlements to greet the victorious soldiers. I shielded my eyes against the bright sun, straining to catch a glimpse of Prince Václav.

At last I could see the mass of soldiers, horses, and carts. Banners waved in the breeze. Sunlight reflected like a swarm of fireflies off metal helmets and weapons. Where was the prince?

Some in the crowd apparently saw him before I did.

"Václav!" they shouted. I joined in the chant. "Václav! Václav!"

From somewhere in the back galloped Prince Václav on his black horse, taking his place in front to lead the army home.

The roar was deafening as we stamped our feet, adding to the voices. We did not stop until the prince had ridden through the gate, followed by his battle chiefs. I watched just long enough to see that camps were being set up in the fields before I ducked and squirmed through the crowd to get to the great hall before Václav did.

I scurried to take my place behind Dragomíra and closest to Přibislava just before the doors opened and the returning heroes entered. Václav strode toward his mother, still wearing his mail and armed with sword and dagger, but he had laid aside his helm and lance.

He smiled at Přibislava and cast a glance at me, it seemed, before he turned to his mother and went down on one knee.

"With the help of the Most High God I have defended the land against its enemies." His voice, almost a shout, rang out clear and strong to everyone in the room.

"Are the Bavarians destroyed, or returned to their own land?" Dragomíra asked.

Václav stood. He was tall enough that he did not have to look up at his mother, even though she sat in a chair raised on the dais. "After fighting for many days, they retreated from our superior forces. There was no need to destroy them."

Boleslav looked as if he wanted to say something, but Dragomíra stayed him. "Do you have proof they returned to Bavaria?" she asked.

Silence hung in the air. Even her loyal *voyvodes* looked shocked that the duchess would so insult the prince.

Václav broke the tension with a laugh. "Did you expect the head of Arnulf for a trophy, Mother?" He shook his head and pulled a scroll from his belt, tossing it on the table between them. "Here is a pledge in Arnulf's own hand not to breach our border again."

Dragomíra picked up the scroll, opened it, and scanned the writing. The prince glanced at me. His eyes twinkled.

"Well done, Václav," the Duchess finally said. "Let the feasting begin."

I silently cheered when Václav sat down, not at the head table with his mother and her loyal followers, but at the lower tables, among his battle chiefs.

I could hardly wait for the feast to end and the wee hours of the night to begin.

Chapter 7

I HURRIED TO THE tower that night, dodging a couple of drunken soldiers who half-heartedly tried to stop me. To my great disappointment, I found the room where I had studied with the prince dimly lit by the moon's faint rays. Quietly I entered and was greeted by a silent Žito, who put his finger to his lips and pointed to the chapel alcove.

There, kneeling in prayer was Prince Václav. He had cast aside his mail and sword belt and put on his black woolen robe. I wanted so badly to speak with him, to hear about his heroic deeds, but I saw no hero now. By the feeble light, he seemed to be weeping.

I felt very much the intruder, and turned to go. Žito did not even look at me as I closed the heavy door behind me and drifted back to the great hall. When I reached it, someone had taken my accustomed sleeping place. I found a dark corner in which to curl up, unnoticed, for the rest of the night.

What was wrong with Prince Václav? Why was he weeping that night, of all nights, when he'd returned a hero? Even the *voyvodes* who had seemed so set against him now spoke of him with respect, albeit grudgingly. Now no one could say that Václav was unfit to rule Bohemia. I'd even overheard some of the nobles whispering against Dragomíra, saying that perhaps it was time she stepped down in favor of the prince, since he was close to being of age.

Still Václav was sorrowful, and it disturbed me to see him so. Though I had seen another side of the prince, maybe I had expected a victorious warrior to act differently. A conqueror, humble? Why? Surely he could not feel remorse for defeating his enemies.

With my thoughts a confused jumble, I merely dozed off and on for the rest of the night. By morning I was stiff and sore, and I spent a miserable day cleaning up after the castle's increased population. At least the soldiers from other villages and castles began to leave, so it appeared life would return to normal soon. That night I went again to the prince's tower. As I approached the door, I saw with relief that a faint light emanated from the crack. Carefully I pushed it open—and saw Žito standing there, head bowed. His presence buoyed me with the courage to enter uninvited. When Žito glanced up at me from under his thick dark brows, he neither smiled nor frowned, but simply nodded. I sighed.

I closed the door as quietly as possible and turned, expecting to see my master and the priests studying. But except for a candle burning in the center, the table was bare. Václav knelt alone in the chapel alcove. He still wore his black woolen robe; the soles of his bare feet were raw and bloody.

Instinctively I hurried toward him, ready to cry out his name in concern, but Žito stopped me with a powerful hand.

"Do not disturb him," whispered the guard.

"But his feet . . ." I began.

"They will heal. He works now to heal his troubled soul."

I did not understand how the prince's soul could be troubled. "But why? What could trouble him after his great victory over the Bavarians?"

Žito shrugged, but I did not hear his answer. I turned to see Václav walking slowly toward us.

"My lord." I fell to my knees. I glanced down toward his feet, but of course I couldn't see the bloodied soles of them now.

"Faithful Poidevin," said Václav. When I looked up, he had a weary smile on his face. "Come to resume your studies, I hope?"

"Yes, my lord," I said, rising when he bade me. "Nothing could keep me from your side."

"Tomorrow," said Václav, "when Father Pavel and Father Balád return, we shall begin where we left off."

"Master," I blurted out before I lost my nerve, "I thought you would be glad that your God gave you the victory. And you didn't even have to kill the duke." Something occurred to me then, and I hoped his sadness wasn't my fault for daring to pray for him. "Your God isn't angry, is he?"

Václav sighed. "Not with you, Poidevin. And I pray he will forgive me for wrestling his angels."

"You wrestle angels?" Did this God's angels take vengeance on people like the demons of the old religion? "Is that what happened to your feet?"

Václav shook his head, and his mouth became grim. "Today I walked barefooted to Levý Hradec and back. It was to do penance."

"Penance?"

"Penance," he explained patiently, "is a poor attempt at payment for sin. I suppose you might say it is an earthly punishment in order to avoid the eternal one."

"B-but," I stammered, "what wrong could you have done?" He was so good, how could he have sinned?

The prince gestured for me to sit across the table from him. He sat down and folded his hands while he collected his thoughts. The candlelight between us illuminated his face in the mostly dark room. To me, he looked like a troubled angel.

Finally the prince glanced up. He seemed to have aged years since he went to face the Bavarians. I know he intended to comfort me, but his sadness made me wish I knew how to comfort him.

"I have always known I must rule Bohemia, but that day seemed far distant, as if it might never come to pass." Václav looked down at his folded hands. "As a boy I often dreamed that I was destined to serve some great purpose in the world. This I supposed might be a calling to the priesthood. I was wrong."

He reached across the table and grabbed my hands as if he needed my support. I did not flinch outwardly, but the pain in his face startled me.

"I misunderstood, Poidevin! I so wanted to devote myself to God by becoming a priest that I blinded myself to any other way of service. The Most High wants my heart and my devoted service, but not as one of his priests."

I saw an instant of alarm on Václav's face. He bowed his head then, and I heard only humility, not fear.

"It is for me to rule Bohemia to the glory of God the Father, his Son, Jesus Christ, and the Holy Spirit. I know that if I trust in my feeble strength, I will fail. But if I can humble myself and search for wisdom and ask for God's grace, I can do this difficult thing." He paused and raised his eyes to meet mine. "I've been wrestling angels, Poidevin, because I do not like having to take another man's life."

I frowned. "You said you didn't kill Duke Arnulf."

Václav shook his head. "Not the duke, but I did kill six of his men in the battle." He leaned his chin against his fist. "I thought that in becoming a ruler of men I could be like the wise, righteous Joseph who ruled second to Pharaoh in Egypt." He looked at me expectantly.

I nodded. "The one who stored up grain during the seven fat years for the seven lean years to come?"

"Very good, Poidevin. You have remembered your lessons."

Václav smiled at me now. "He was a true leader of men, but as far as I know, he did not shed men's blood." His smile faded. "Apparently I will have to be a warrior like Joshua instead of a peaceful Joseph, and that is why I wrestle angels."

He grew silent, dropping his head to his hands.

There were many things I wanted to tell the prince. He was the strongest person I had ever met. Already he was like Joseph in his wisdom and kindness. I wanted to tell him I had never known anyone with his kind of courage and humility.

"My lord," I finally said. He looked at me with such patience and genuine concern, even in the midst of his soul-searching, that I felt moved to show my devotion to him. I slid off the wooden bench and came around to kneel beside him on the rush-strewn floor. I placed my right fist over my heart.

"My lord, Václav, I pledge my life in service to you and to your God."

With tears of joy in his eyes, he laid his strong hands on my bony shoulders and squeezed them affectionately. He knelt beside me and bowed his head, praying that I might come to know his God, as he did. In that moment I truly knew what kind of master I had.

Chapter 8

THE FOLLOWING NIGHT before resuming our studies, I accompanied Václav and Father Pavel to a building within the castle walls I had never entered before. Since coming to power, Duchess Dragomíra had kept the main doors of St. George's Basilica locked, but my master had a key to a back entrance. The three of us wore cloaks with hoods to conceal our identities, but the cloudy sky was so dark not even the sleepy night guard noticed us.

When we entered the tomblike church, the air was still and musty from disuse. Father Pavel fumbled in the dark and lit a candle. Then he began to make mysterious preparations in a side room while Václav explained that his mother had outlawed the worship of the Christian God in this holy place.

"As soon as I am crowned, the doors of all the churches will be open again," he said quietly.

My master beckoned me to pray with him at the altar rail, but I could not concentrate. I was curious about what Father Pavel was doing, and heard the splash of water in between his quiet footsteps.

At last the priest returned and without a word we followed him to the side room in which a stone basin had been filled half-way with water. Several candles provided some light. Father Pavel told me to remove my tunic, which I did, and then he helped me up the three stone steps in order to enter the basin. I shivered when my bare skin came in contact with the cold water.

Thankfully Father Pavel spoke in Čech so I could understand his words, though at the time I didn't fully understand their significance. Then after I renounced the devil and confessed my faith in God, the priest baptized me in the name of the Father, the Son, and the Holy Spirit. Father Pavel helped me back down the steps, and Václav wrapped me in a cloth so I could dry myself. I glanced at his face, and to my surprise his cheeks glistened with tears. Only then did I begin to understand that something life-changing had happened.

"Your new life in Christ has begun," my master said with a smile. "Now we are truly brothers."

I quickly dried off and pulled on my tunic, and the three of us donned our cloaks to return to Václav's tower.

⁂

For several weeks my life fell into a happy rhythm. Each day my mistress, Dragomíra, divided my time between her needs and those of her sweet daughter, at least in those duties appropriate for a slave boy to perform for a noble lady: fetching firewood, keeping the fire going, cleaning out the ashes, delivering food and messages. That is how I came to know Přibislava better. I spent every night in study with my master and the priests. The more I learned about Václav's God, the more I understood the source of the Prince's goodness. I could see why this triune God, so different from the fearful gods and evil spirits that inhabited Bohemia's forests, inspired my master to such loyalty.

However, one question continued to trouble me. I did not understand how the God of the goodly Václav could allow such terrible suffering in the world, and most especially the suffering of good and innocent people. On more than one occasion I came close to framing the question on my tongue in order to ask my master and the priests, but cowardice melted the words like the snow melted each spring. Did I fear their answer might uproot the seedling of my faith? Somehow I had to find a way to ask the question.

But my opportunity vanished, for on Midsummer's Eve, my second in Castle Praha, everything changed.

The feast began like any other. Dragomíra sat in the center of the head table, with Boleslav seated on her left and Přibislava between Boleslav and Václav. On her right, instead of the usual Tunna and Gommon, two other *voyvodes* had earned the duchess's favor on this festive occasion. The older man sat hunched over his food, but the younger one drank freely of the wine. He cuffed me, and I almost dropped the platter of meats I carried.

"More wine, boy." He held up his goblet.

I glanced at my mistress to see what she would say.

"Even my best servants cannot do two things at once," she snapped. "You will have more wine when the boy has finished serving our meat."

The man glared at me as I moved down the table. It was a relief to finally serve Přibislava and Václav. The warmth of their friendly faces gave me courage. I took the empty platter to the kitchen and exchanged it for a wineskin. It was nearly full and difficult to manage, so I took greater care than usual pouring wine for the sullen *voyvode*. Unfortunately, just as I lined up the neck of the skin with the goblet and started to pour, the older man sneezed, startling me. Wine splashed onto the younger man's robe.

"Clumsy fool!" he shouted. He jumped to his feet and drew a jeweled dagger from his belt. "We should use this one as the sacrifice tonight." He grabbed the front of my tunic and held the blade to my throat.

"Hold!" Dragomíra rose from her chair. Václav stood also, but he did not speak. The *voyvode* glared at them both as my mistress continued. "Release my servant and leave my presence at once, or face the consequences."

The man seemed about to refuse when Boleslav spoke up. "We can't use him for the sacrifice," he said. "Tonight we offer Ladislav's finest bull. This slave will have to wait until the winter solstice."

Though Boleslav's words made me sick with fear, they did reach the *voyvode* before he used his knife on me. He let go my tunic, sheathed his knife, and stormed from the hall.

Dragomíra reseated herself, but Václav continued to stand.

"Brother," said Boleslav, "are you planning to join us this evening?" He grinned as if they shared a secret.

Václav crossed his arms. "You know that I will not." He spoke to the duchess. "I shall take my leave of you now." He nodded to Přibislava and stepped down from their table.

"Václav," said Dragomíra. He glanced back. "All loyal Čechs are occupied at the bonfires tonight."

The prince turned to face his mother. I inwardly cheered the determination in his face. "I follow the one true God, and he demands no sacrifice of blood, for he has already sent his only begotten Son, the Lord Jesus Christ, to die for our sins."

Boleslav snickered. "And you say you do not believe in human sacrifice."

Dragomíra's face grew red. "I forbid you to leave."

"I will not stay, Mother. This must come to an end."

As he left the room, I wondered what it was that Václav wanted to end. Did he mean his conversation with the duchess, or something much larger?

As soon as the revelers left for the bonfires, I rushed through my cleanup chores and hurried to check on my master. I saw when I reached his rooms that there were to be no lessons this night.

"Poidevin." Václav's robe swirled at his feet as he approached me.

"Yes, my lord?" When I knelt before him, he raised me up.

"I am about to ask a hard thing of you."

"What is it, Master?" At that moment I could have gone into the lion's den for him, as Daniel had.

Václav chuckled at my shining enthusiasm. Before he spoke again, his eyes became somber. "I must travel through Bohemia and visit with the people. I need to discover who my supporters are, and perhaps win over those who are not."

That seemed a good thing to do, now that he'd proven his mettle as a battle commander.

"I am nearly old enough to claim the crown," he continued, looking away, "yet I fear my mother shall not easily give up the power she wields. I need the approval of as many *voyvodes* as I can find."

Žito spoke up for the first time. "You will find more support among the people than you realize, my lord."

"I pray you are right, Žito," Václav said. "But whatever the case, we will soon find out."

He turned his attention back to me. "Would that I could take you with me, Poidevin, for the priests cannot come for our nightly sessions while I am away. I may be gone for weeks or even months, but I must leave you here."

"But, but . . ." My heart began to flop about like a fish out of water. "I can go with you, Master. I can serve you as I have the duchess."

Václav shook his head, and I saw regret in his eyes. "I need you here, to be my eyes and ears while I am gone." He squeezed my shoulder. "Will you do this for me, Poidevin?"

What could I say? The last thing in the world I wanted was for him to leave me alone with Dragomíra and Boleslav and their loyal followers.

"Yes, my lord," I whispered, trying to sound braver than I felt. I hoped my mistress would let me continue to serve Přibislava, at least. She alone was most like her goodly brother.

"God will keep you safe while Žito and I are absent from you," he said.

I swallowed as fear tightened its cold fingers around my heart. I could only hope he was right.

Chapter 9

ITHOUT VÁCLAV'S TEMPERING influence, Dragomíra grew more and more ruthless. She raised taxes on the peasants, passed even stricter laws punishing the followers of Václav's God, and found arbitrary reasons to confiscate property and possessions from the most innocent of people. Because she handsomely rewarded her loyal followers, they became more loyal and more bold. I feared that one more clumsy incident in the presence of the court might lead to the addition of my head on a pike at the castle gate.

Přibislava found me alone one day in her mother's rooms while I scrubbed the floor. She cradled a roll of vellum.

"There you are, Poidevin," she said. "I've been looking for you."

I stopped scrubbing and wiped my hands on my tunic. "And why would my lady be looking for me?" I asked. I couldn't help but notice how her dark plaits contrasted with the cream color of her gown. She seemed to have blossomed from little girl to young woman overnight.

Přibislava lowered her dark lashes. "I saw you reading one of my brother's scrolls the other day."

My heart faltered in its beating. Had she caught me sneaking up to Václav's rooms? "Why, my lady, what do you mean?"

She raised her eyes to mine. "You don't have to pretend with me, Poidevin. I know my brother has been teaching you to read."

"What makes you think so?" I frowned. Would she report that to her mother?

She shrugged. "Oh, I just know." The princess placed her delicate hand on my arm, just for a moment. "But I would never betray you. Surely you know that?"

I cleared my throat. "So now you are reading my mind?"

She swatted my arm, and I fell, pretending to be injured.

"Did I hurt you, Poidevin?" Her brows furrowed in concern.

"Oh, my lady," I groaned. "You do not know your own strength."

We laughed together then.

Her smile faded, and the princess stared at me with pleading in her eyes. "Would you please read this letter from my brother?"

I took the roll of vellum to the table and spread it open. There was a second, smaller roll within it that I laid aside. Přibislava stood beside me, trying to decipher the Latin inscription.

"My dearest sister," I read aloud. "God has richly blessed me, and I hope all is well with you. I wanted you to know that it will be some time before I can return. Be of good courage, sister, and trust in God with all your heart. He will triumph in the end.

"Since Poidevin is surely reading this to you, I send him my greetings as well. Both of you watch out for the other. God grant that I will see you before the winter.

"With great affection, your brother, Václav."

Then I opened the smaller piece of vellum but did not read it aloud, for it began, "To my brother in plenty as well as famine." I frowned. Was my master speaking about Joseph? Was this his way to keep the letter private, even if it fell into the wrong hands? I continued reading.

"More and more people understand the importance of turning from the famine of God's word to the hope of life, both here and in the life to come. Rejoice with me, for it will not be long before the years of famine end and the blessed years of plenty begin."

I puzzled over the words, but it appeared to me that my master was gathering support among the people in order to take the throne and bring the knowledge of God to all Bohemia.

Přibislava remained silent the entire time I pondered this second message. "I wish Václav would teach me how to read," she finally said, "but Mother would never allow it."

"I suppose I could teach you," I said.

Přibislava caught her breath and gazed at me, hopeful. Finally she shook her head. "No, Poidevin. I will not endanger you."

After that, I knew I had an ally in Přibislava, at least in most matters. I did not want to endanger her, however, by sharing with her the charge Václav had given to me. I trusted no one, but merely listened and marked all I heard as either for or against my master.

When the weather turned colder and the leaves changed from green to bright shades of red and gold, Přibislava had a visitor. The lady was a little older than she, closer to Václav's age, the daughter of a powerful *voyvode* whom Dragomíra was trying to influence. I heard the girl's name before I saw her: Ana. She was to spend the winter at the castle as a companion for Přibislava.

"Boy," Dragomíra said, staring at me with her cold dark eyes. "Since you have proven yourself trustworthy to me as well as to Přibislava, you will act as a manservant for our visitor's needs for as long as she remains. Serve her as you have my daughter."

I solemnly bowed, grateful to break eye contact with her. Inwardly I cheered. Perhaps now I would spend even less time in the presence of Dragomíra and Boleslav. Of course, it would give me less opportunity to hear things of value to my master. But as winter approached, the season of the bloodthirsty goddess Morana, I could not help but fear being chosen for a human sacrifice. I wondered if I would always feel such dread about the coming of the winter solstice.

For a while, at least, I could be distracted by Přibislava and her new friend.

When I first saw Ana, her father was presenting her to my mistress. The girl kept her eyes lowered and meekly curtsied to the duchess. Her long braids were amber, almost the color of honey, and her skin was smooth with a faint blush. I was afraid Prince Boleslav would notice how pretty she was, but fortunately he was angry about something and saw only that his cup was empty.

"More wine, boy," he growled, kicking me when I did not respond quickly enough.

I took his cup and refilled it, and by the time I turned back, Ana had retired with Přibislava. I was glad Dragomíra sent me to attend them, because Boleslav's ugly mood only portended ill for me should I remain in the hall.

I found the girls giggling together as they walked down the passageway toward Přibislava's room. They didn't notice me until they'd reached the heavy wooden door.

"Allow me," I said, rushing to open it.

Startled, Ana whirled and stared at me with big brown eyes. *They were doe's eyes*, I thought, *with long lashes.* "Who are you?" she asked in a lilting voice.

Přibislava placed a hand on the girl's arm and smiled. "Don't be alarmed. This is Poidevin, our servant. He is most trustworthy."

"My ladies," I said with a bow. Then I opened the door and stepped back to let them enter first.

"Oh, Přibi," Ana said, "your room is so grand!"

I could not help but notice how graceful the girl's movements were. A thought entered my head: What if this girl with the glorious honey hair was still here when my master returned? Might he notice her, too?

The first snows fell, and I found myself imagining that I had become a bodyguard for the two girls, like Žito was to the prince, and surely just as indispensable. At least I was spending more time with Přibislava and her friend and less time in the company of Boleslav.

In my newly imagined role as bodyguard, I also found myself drawn more and more to the castle yard to watch the soldiers practicing archery or fighting in mock combat with sword and battle-ax. If I was to be a proper bodyguard, I would need to be armed with a dagger, at least. Perhaps when my master and Žito came back I would muster the courage to ask him about that.

Prince Václav finally returned to Praha just before the winter solstice. While Dragomíra, Boleslav, and their pagan nobles were feasting, Václav entered the great hall, his fur-lined mantle dusted with snow. I stopped in my tracks in the middle of serving the duchess from a plate of meats. My master had grown taller, his hair longer, and the beginnings of a moustache and beard darkened his boyish face. Our eyes met briefly in silent acknowledgement as he strode toward his mother at the head table.

"Greetings, Mother," he said. He nodded to a sullen Boleslav and smiled at Přibislava, but he did not seem to notice the lovely Ana beside her.

"Václav," said Dragomíra with a sigh. "You have a fine sense of timing. Will you join us in our feasting?" She gestured to the table.

"I think not," he said, "knowing what it is you celebrate. I only wished to inform you that I have returned for a short time. While I am here, I think it prudent that we discuss some things in private."

Dragomíra frowned. "There is nothing you must say to me privately that you cannot speak before my council."

Václav leaned toward her, his eyes blazing with fervor. "Your regency will not last forever, Mother. Your council will not remain as my council. There are matters you and I must discuss, or there shall be consequences."

Boleslav slammed his goblet on the table, and I flinched. "Do not presume to threaten the lawful regent of Bohemia."

My master ignored his brother, speaking directly to Dragomíra. "I do not threaten, Mother. I do, however, insist you remember that the time for my coronation grows ever closer." He nodded to her. "When you are finished here, I request a private conference with you."

Before Dragomíra could reply, Václav turned and strode from the room. Several *voyvodes* made a discreet exit, following him. The rest turned their attention to the duchess to see how she would react.

I thought Dragomíra's face might burst. Even Boleslav held his tongue while in such proximity to her brewing storm of rage.

"Boy," she said, snaring me with her eyes, "take Přibislava and Lady Ana back to their rooms." She stood and pointed to the door. "All of you servants, leave at once." While we hurried to obey, one of the *voyvodes* closed the heavy doors behind us.

After I helped the distraught girls settle themselves in Přibislava's room, I hurried to Václav's tower, praying that I could speak with him. To my dismay there was no one there. I sagged against the door, wondering what to do, when Žito stepped out of the shadows, startling me.

"Peace, my friend," he said. "I have sent our master away and must follow him at once."

"But why?" This news drained what little courage I had remaining.

"Because the time is not yet ripe, and for him to remain here will only jeopardize his safety." Zito's dark eyes blazed.

I nodded, not really understanding. Of course I did not want my master to be endangered.

"What about me?" I sounded pitiful, even to myself.

Žito placed a heavy hand on my bony shoulder. "You must be brave and not draw attention to yourself. Přibislava needs you now more than ever."

I sighed, knowing he was right, even though I wanted with all my being to go with him and Prince Václav. "Will you come back?"

Žito grimaced, the closest thing to a smile I'd ever seen on his face. "Have faith, Poidevin." He turned and left me. I felt more alone than ever in this castle filled with evil.

Chapter 10

ORTUNATELY, THE SEVERE winter prevented Dragomíra from making any great effort to find the prince. But because of the terrible weather, there were extra sacrifices made to pacify the goddess Morana.

"Why don't you sacrifice him?" Boleslav asked Dragomíra one evening. They sat around the fire in her room with a group of *voyvodes*. All eyes turned to me. Fear leaped to my throat.

Dragomíra laughed. "He is too useful to me. We have plenty of orphans for sacrifices."

A crafty look gleamed in Boleslav's eyes. "But, Mother, perhaps Morana continues with this weather because you have only offered worthless sacrifices. If you were to offer her something of value, then perhaps she would take our sacrifices more seriously."

"Then perhaps I should offer you, my son," the Duchess said.

I didn't dare laugh. But Ladislav, the eldest among the *voyvodes*, did. "I think you need not worry about making such a sacrifice, my lady." His eyes twinkled as he drank from his cup. I wondered if he really meant that Boleslav was not of great value, but of course, even Ladislav would not be so bold as to say words like those aloud.

That evening was one of the few in which I found myself in the presence of all the faithful followers of my mistress. I counted myself fortunate in that I was allowed to spend most of my time with Přibislava and her friend, trying to keep them as comfortable as possible. Whenever I tended their fire, I thought of my master and hoped he had found a warm place somewhere in Bohemia. I worried about what would happen to him, about what would happen to us all.

One especially cold day I brought more firewood to Přibislava's room. She and Ana sat huddled together, wrapped in furs, and did not notice me until I added my load of wood to the small pile beside the hearth.

"Poidevin," said Přibislava, "I've been waiting for you." Her smile roused my curiosity.

I wiped my bare hands on my breeches and then tucked them under my arms to warm them. "How may I be of service, my lady?" Though my teeth managed not to chatter too badly, it was difficult to keep my jaw still. Every muscle in my body wanted to shiver, it seemed.

With her gloved hand Přibislava plucked a scroll from beneath her fur blanket. She spoke quietly. "I've received another letter from my brother. Will you read it aloud, Poidevin?"

Eagerly I chose the letter over warm hands and quickly unrolled the vellum, laying it flat upon the nearby table.

"My dear sister," I read. "I pray this missive finds you warm and in good health. Although winter threatens never to leave, spring is coming soon. Revive your weary spirit, dearest sister, just as most of the people of Bohemia have done. Spring will bring new life and a new birth of faith. The thirst for knowledge will be quenched in the waters of truth, and the darkness of ignorance and fear will be banished, never again to reign over our people.

"Since I feel certain Poidevin is reading this to you, reassure him that all goes well, even better than we could have hoped for.

"I plan to see you before the daisies bloom on the hills. May God bless you and keep you in his care until we meet again.

"Your affectionate brother, Václav."

I heard Přibislava's sigh and glanced up to see a glow of contentment on her face. Ana looked thoughtful at the words of Václav. Before either of them spoke, I scanned the vellum for a possible private message to me, but it seemed my master intended for me to recognize the deeper meaning behind his words to Přibislava. I looked at her again.

"There is nothing now to fear, Poidevin," she said. "When he comes back, my brother will right all wrongs."

I nodded to show her I understood, but I did not feel I could speak openly of the message in front of Ana. My master's safety was too important to take unnecessary risks.

※

At last the days grew longer and the deep snows began to melt. The river overflowed its banks, and I spent many hours scrubbing mud from the walkways where people had tracked it in.

One cloudless morning the sun appeared, and birds sang in greeting. As I ran past Bora's hut, I waved to her while she worked in her garden. She grinned and waved back.

The moment I entered the castle, a guard cuffed me, knocking me to the ground.

"Your mistress is looking for you," he growled.

I scampered away before he could kick me. Did he mean Přibislava or the duchess? To be safe, I ran to Dragomíra's rooms first. Grim-faced, she stood beside her table. Two scrolls lay next to a burning candle, one sealed and the other not. The duchess ordered me to find Boleslav and her faithful *voyvodes*. I spent the next half hour running from room to room, collecting them. As soon as they were all present, Dragomíra dismissed me.

After the door closed, I heard the sound of someone barring it. I had thought to go down to the kitchen, but a nagging sense of dread impelled me to attempt a dangerous mission.

I ran down the hall and took the tower steps two at a time in my haste to reach the courtyard. There were few people about at this time of day. Most traded in the city, worked the fields, or went about their business in and around the castle. I prayed no one would notice me.

One guard stood up on the tower, but he was looking out at the countryside beyond. Quickly I backed up to the wall just below Dragomíra's rooms, making sure the guard was still turned away, and I began to climb up the thick vines. Fear must have given me strength, because it only took moments to reach the window of my mistress's bedchamber. Silently I pulled myself over the stone ledge and into the room. I calmed myself so no one would hear my panting. I crept closer to the sitting room, where I was sure Dragomíra and her conspirators were plotting something.

"Won't there be resistance?" one *voyvode* was asking.

"Not armed resistance," Dragomíra said, "especially when we tell them it was Václav's decision. The scroll with his seal should be proof enough for any doubter."

I heard Boleslav's sneering voice. "It's only natural he should want to enter a monastery. He would rather pray to his God than eat. He gives his own food and clothing to worthless beggars and walks barefooted over sharp rocks just to inflict pain on himself."

"Silence, Boleslav," Dragomíra said. "His religious fervor is evident to all. His leaving will cause no alarm."

"When shall we take him?" asked the deep voice of Ladislav.

"I have received word that Václav is returning today," said Dragomíra. "Tonight will be soon enough."

"What about Přibislava?" Boleslav asked. "Won't she warn him?"

"I am sending Přibislava away with the daughter of Žibrid," Dragomíra said. "She will not interfere."

I had heard enough. With trembling hands I lowered myself to the ground. Somehow I had to warn Prince Václav.

Chapter 11

*I*RAN DOWN THE road away from Praha as fast as my legs could carry me. Twice I looked behind me to see the castle on the hill growing smaller. Noticing a gnarled tree beside the road, set apart from any others, I took an apple out of my tunic and offered it to the spirit that guarded the tree. Only then did I climb to a high branch where I could watch for Václav without being seen. I was used to living indoors, and did not feel safe around large trees. One tree was bad enough, but a whole forest of them possessed by evil spirits could combine their power and do unspeakable things. My faith was still in its infancy then. Because Václav and I had not yet discussed the old superstitions, I had not discarded the pagan rituals I had practiced from childhood.

As the sun climbed toward midday, my mouth felt dry, and I realized I had had no food or water since the day before. I began to feel a little foolish about giving away my only apple to a spirit I wasn't even sure existed.

I forced my thoughts away from hunger and thirst and concentrated instead on warning the prince to stay well away from Praha. This time, I intended to convince him to take me with him. I could no longer pretend to serve Dragomíra when my loyalty was with Václav, at least not in a way anyone would believe.

I watched the road so intently that when I saw two riders approaching, I almost didn't recognize them. I nearly fell in my haste to scramble down the tree.

"Master! Žito!" I cried, running toward them. My joy was mingled with fear, and I'm certain I looked quite insane.

"Poidevin!" Václav halted his horse and jumped down. "What is the matter?"

I fell to my knees. "They are plotting to take you if you go to the castle, my lord," I managed to say. "The duchess even sent Přibislava and her friend away so they couldn't warn you."

Václav knelt in front of me and gripped my shoulders. He waited until I looked up into his gray eyes. Then he stood, raising me up. With a start I realized I had grown almost as tall as my master.

"The time has come, Žito," he said, without turning to look at his faithful guard.

"Yes, my lord." Žito wheeled his horse around and rode back the way they'd come.

"I'm coming with you," I blurted out.

Václav shook his head. "Not this time. It is too dangerous. However," and he held up a hand to silence my protest, "I have an important task for you."

"What is it, Master?" I asked, disappointed.

"You must find a way to keep the castle servants out of harm's way without alerting your mistress." He placed a hand on my shoulder.

My face must have shown my confusion because Václav grinned. "I know I can entrust their safety to you, Poidevin."

"You mean, you aren't going away?"

The prince slowly shook his head. "It is time for change in Bohemia."

I straightened beneath his hand, trying to project some of the confidence he'd placed in me. "I will do my best, my lord."

"Then I will see you shortly." He mounted his horse and galloped away. Though I trusted my master with all my heart, still I felt a stab of fear. Had he found enough loyal Čechs to take the throne? Wresting power from Dragomíra would not be easy.

I found Bora first. She promised to bar the door and stay inside the hut with her husband. Handling the other servants was more of a problem, because I did not know how many were loyal to Dragomíra despite their complaints.

"There's to be a feast tonight," I announced to the cook and his scullions.

"I heard no such news." Cook crossed his arms over his stained apron.

"That's because my mistress only now decided to have it," I said.

I ducked the blow that Cook leveled at my head and continued as if nothing had happened.

"My lady desires roast boar and a brace of partridges, fresh bread, and one of your confections." I chose dishes that would keep the most people in the kitchen for the longest time.

Cook glared at me, but he gestured to one of the bakers. "Well, you heard the boy. Get to work."

Before he could strike at me again, I fled.

Later that day, Dragomíra, Boleslav, and their loyal *voyvodes* met in the great hall. My mistress did not seem surprised at the quantity of food. Knowing her as I did, perhaps I'd correctly anticipated that she would want to publicly celebrate Prince Václav's imminent departure to the monastery. She had certainly dressed to celebrate, wearing a bold red dress and matching veil glittering with jewels.

In contrast to the pleasant music, Boleslav looked murderous. He could scarcely contain his impatience to be rid of Václav. I could not fathom why he hated his brother so much. He must have a heart of stone to despise Václav's goodness.

I had heard nothing from either my master or Žito, so my imagination toyed with all manner of disaster. My carelessness proved nearly fatal when I jarred Boleslav's elbow, causing him to splash the contents of his goblet all over his red and black tunic.

"Cursed slave!" he shouted, backhanding me with such force that I fell to the rushes. "I've suffered enough of your clumsiness."

He leaped from his seat, drawing his dagger and raising it over my head.

"Boleslav, hold!" There was anger in Dragomíra's voice, but I don't believe it came from concern for my fate.

The music stopped. We heard shouting and the clash of swords just outside the hall.

Dragomíra stood up. "What is going on?" she demanded.

Before anyone could answer, the doors slammed back. I gasped when I saw my master, with Žito beside him, leading scores of armed warriors. Václav cut a princely figure wearing his father's red ducal robe and a circlet of gold on his brow. He had drawn his sword. Blood dulled the blade. I shivered, not from cold but from fear. Boleslav's knife was inches away, poised to strike me. What would happen to me if I grabbed his wrist and turned the blade?

My master walked calmly toward Dragomíra's table, his eyes never leaving her face. The duchess puffed up like a toad trying to bluff a cat that has cornered it.

"How dare you shed the blood of your countrymen in my castle?"

"I only shed blood in self-defense, Mother," Václav said. "You, on the other hand, murder innocent old women at their prayers and plot to rid yourself of your own son and lawful heir."

Gasps and whispers filled the silence as Václav and Dragomíra stared at one another. Finally the duchess broke the impasse with a nervous laugh.

"All your sleepless nights have made you mad, Václav. How can you fail to see the folly of your religion? You can no longer tell the difference between what is real and what exists only in your own mind."

"Enough, Mother!" At his command, Dragomíra stopped her raving. I felt Boleslav tense his body beside me, although what he thought he might accomplish against a room full of armed soldiers, I did not know. "I cannot allow you to continue to rule Bohemia. You make laws injurious to her loyal subjects and plot assassinations with your nobles. The time has come for you to step down. I now claim my inherited right to rule over this land."

I refrained from cheering. Boleslav still stood over me, gripping the knife.

For several moments no one moved or spoke. I began to fear that Dragomíra would resist.

"Well, Mother," my master said at last, "will you step down graciously, or must I use force against you and your *voyvodes*?"

Dragomíra turned her head and looked at the men beside her. Each inclined his head, bowing to her decision. All, of course, except Boleslav.

"Don't let this weakling induce you to step down," he snarled. "He lacks the will to use force against anyone."

Václav shook his head and took a step closer, turning his attention to Boleslav for the first time. "How little you under-stand me, brother. My strength comes from the Lord, and he has given me victory over my enemies. Don't make yourself one of them, unless you believe you can fight against God."

Boleslav shifted the knife in his hand and hurled it at Václav. Žito threw himself in front of our master, deflecting the knife with his shield.

"Seize them," Václav said.

"Wait!" Dragomíra reached out to grip Boleslav's wrist. She turned to her younger son and spoke in a voice that only he and I could hear. "We have lost this day, my son," she whispered. "You must wait and watch. Another day will come, one on which Bohemia will belong to you."

Boleslav jerked his head, but he would not look at her eyes.

"Today, I concede to you, Václav," Dragomíra held her head high, full of pride to the end.

My master stepped up to the table. His glance included each of Dragomíra's loyal *voyvodes* standing beside her. "Now I am Duke of Bohemia and Prince of all Čechs," he said. "Let it be known to all that Duke Václav will no longer tolerate the pagan policies of Dragomíra's regency."

He looked at his mother and brother. "Let no one ever again be found guilty of the crime of murder. If the fear of God does not keep you from transgressing the law, know that my wrath will come down upon such evildoers."

After a pause to let his words echo in the ears of all present, Václav turned to include his faithful soldiers. "May the love of peace at home and abroad rule our land. Let justice reign to the glory of God!"

The men erupted in a cheer as I slipped under the table to stand beside my master. Dragomíra's shoulders sagged, but Boleslav scowled. What could Václav do with him?

Chapter 12

THE FATES OF Boleslav and Dragomíra had to wait until after the coronation, set for seven days hence. Přibislava returned, and so did her friend Ana. With all the preparations and the steady stream of visitors, my master paid no attention to the young lady with the long honey braids.

The coronation day began before dawn in the kitchens, as Cook and his helpers started to prepare a mountain of food. When I ran up to the castle wall to greet the morning, the roads were already full of people. It appeared nearly everyone in the land walked, rode a horse, or filled a wagon on the way to Praha to celebrate the crowning of the new duke.

On that day the great hall had a festive appearance. The banners of every tribe hung from the rafters. Local bards laid aside their rivalry for the day in order to fill the hall with music. Even Bora wore an embroidered apron over her dress and a new scarf on her head.

My master spent the morning at his altar in prayer. He neither ate nor spoke. He seemed at times to shake with fear, and exhibited a humility at odds with his triumphant show of force against Dragomíra the week before.

"Master," I finally said, unable to keep from speaking to him, "the time approaches. Your people await you."

He turned toward me, his face pale. "Forgive me, Poidevin. You are right. I should not keep the people waiting." When he rose from his knees, he seemed taller. Perhaps, though, it was only that I saw him as even greater than before.

I helped Václav dress in a simple, white linen tunic and slippers. Buckling on his empty sword belt over the tunic, he laid a hand on my shoulder. "Thank you, Poidevin."

"For what, my lord?"

"Your presence is a blessing to me."

I felt my face become hot, so to hide my embarrassment and joy, I went down on one knee, grabbed his hand, and pressed it to my forehead.

"Most noble Václav," I began, but my throat closed over the rest I had intended to say.

There was a knock at the door. Father Pavel opened it and entered quietly. The priest wore snow white robes and a gold crucifix. His hands trembled with excitement.

"If only my grandmother were alive to see this day," Václav sighed.

"Rest assured, my son, our sainted Ludmila is watching with great joy."

I saw a peace come over my master's face, erasing his tension and distress, and I was glad for it.

Father Pavel held out his hand, and Václav crossed the room to take it, bending one knee, as I had just done.

"Pray for me, Father, that I might be a wise and godly ruler over my people." His voice was husky with emotion.

I lowered my eyes while the priest prayed, partly in Slavonic and partly in Latin. When my master rose, I followed the two of them down the steps to the waiting crowds.

❧

The procession wound down the hill to the gates of the city of Praha so Václav could lead the people back up to St. George's

Basilica. It occurred to me that Václav was like Saint George. He, too, had slain an evil dragon, the pagan rule that held our people hostage. My master looked the part of the saintly knight as he rode on a white stallion, followed by his retinue on foot. As he passed the crowds lining the narrow streets of Praha, the people waved and cheered. They fell in behind us, flowing like a great sea toward the church.

Upon arriving at St. George's, Václav dismounted and entered. On the benches crowded the *voyvodes* from all of Bohemia, as well as Germanic nobles and those from other duchies to the north. Father Pavel and several other priests stood at the altar with a Germanic bishop wearing his jeweled cope and miter. One priest held a red fur-lined robe, another a golden scepter, a third the new crown on a satin pillow.

I squeezed in between two soldiers against the back wall and watched my master process up the aisle. His back was straight and proud, but not for himself. He had asked the priests to crown him so all Bohemia would know that their duke followed the Christian God.

There was silence in the crowded church when Václav reached the altar steps and stood facing the bishop and priests.

"Who is it that approaches the altar of the Lord?" Father Pavel called out in a clear voice, speaking not in Latin, but in the language of the Čechs.

"I am Václav, son of Vratislav, the son of Bořivoj, of the dynasty Přemyslid. I have come to claim the birthright of my family."

Žito brought forward a wooden plow that once belonged to Přemysl himself. By choosing this item of his ancestor as part of the coronation regalia, Václav wanted to show that he intended to rule as a peaceful and humble servant.

My master knelt as the bishop began his litany in Latin. Václav was admonished to lead Bohemia in the fear of God. His head was anointed with oil, as the biblical kings David and Solomon of old had been anointed.

One of the priests draped the heavy robe across my master's shoulders. Another placed the scepter in his hand. At last, the new crown was brought forward.

"Václav, son of Vratislav, son of Bořivoj, I give you this token of your supreme royalty." As Father Pavel set the crown upon my master's dark hair, a ray of sunlight struck the gold and jewels with a brilliant flash, almost as if God himself had given his approval.

"Rise, Václav, Duke of Bohemia and Prince of the Čechs."

My master rose and slowly turned to face his people. Wearing the robe and crown, with the scepter cradled in his arm, he looked so regal that my heart could not contain my joy. I added my voice to the shouts of every person in the church. The sound reverberated in the vaulted ceiling and rose up to heaven:

"Václav! Václav!"

Chapter 13

As the procession prepared to return to the castle for a celebration banquet, a horseman forced his way through the crowd all the way to the stone steps of the church. The moment Václav stepped through the doorway, the man slid down from his trembling, frothing horse and knelt at my master's feet. His mantle was worn and dirty.

"Your Grace," said the horseman. As the man pulled off his sweaty cap before raising his gaze to the new duke, I could see the fear in his eyes.

Václav held up his hand to silence the excited chatter of the crowd. "Who are you?"

"I am Jan, a blacksmith from Svatava, near the western border, and your humble servant."

"It appears that you have most urgent news, Jan," Václav said.

"Your Grace," the smith began, swallowing, "a great army approaches from the northwest."

"An army? Whose?" Václav glanced over at his mother and brother. They stood between the guards who had insured they would witness the coronation. Dragomíra's face blanched, but Boleslav could not contain a triumphant smirk.

Surely they did not have enough loyal followers to attack a duke at his coronation?

"They are Germanic warriors," Jan continued. "We have fled before their advance, and I was chosen to ride ahead and warn you."

"A Germanic army?" Václav stared at his mother.

"Yes, my lord."

"Led by whom?" Václav asked in a cold voice.

The smith trembled. "King Henry the Fowler of Saxony leads them, Your Grace."

The crowd gasped and began to whisper fearfully. Boleslav sneered at his brother. Václav strode toward him and Dragomíra. Even the guards took a step back.

"What do you know of this, Mother?" asked Václav. "Why would King Henry invade Bohemia at this time?"

Dragomíra glanced around, looking for support. She seemed smaller in her captivity, as if all power had been drained from her. Now, without her office, she was just a tired, aging woman.

"The Fowler demanded that Bohemia pay him tribute," she finally said.

"Of course, we refused," said Boleslav. "Bohemia will not bow to any Germanic king. We would rather fight and die than be subject to foreigners!"

Many close by who heard Boleslav's cry echoed it. Not an hour had passed since Václav's coronation and my master was already confronting his first crisis.

Václav turned back to Jan, who had not moved from his knees.

"Where is the Fowler's army now?"

"Within two days' march, my lord."

"How large is this army?"

Jan swept the large crowd with his arm. "I would estimate at least this many on horse, thrice that number on foot, plus wagons."

More gasps and whispers passed through the crowd.

Václav turned toward the *voyvodes*, who stood huddled together at the entrance to the church.

"We must meet at once in the hall of judgment. Decisions must be made, decisions that will affect us all." He glanced again at his mother and Boleslav.

The new duke removed his crown and passed it to Father Pavel. He shrugged out of the glorious robe.

"Bring them, Žito." He nodded to Dragomíra and Boleslav. "We have work to do."

Václav mounted his great white horse and caught my gaze, beckoning for me to follow. "I need you, Poidevin."

Straightening my shoulders, I pushed past the richly dressed *voyvodes* and followed my master back to the castle.

Once in the great hall the trestle tables were pushed against the walls to make room for the *voyvodes* and as many soldiers as possible to fit inside. Václav seated himself in his father's great wooden throne and allowed Father Pavel to place the crown back on his head.

"We don't have much time," said my master, "so I will make this brief."

He signaled the guards to bring Dragomíra and Boleslav forward. Žito approached from the back of the room, herding two men. I did not recognize them at first because they were bound and gagged. Then I saw that they were Tunna and Gommon, the men who had risen to favor with the duchess after they'd murdered Václav's grandmother. Their elegant clothing was soiled, and they glared at Václav with open contempt.

"My first judgment as Duke of Bohemia is to pass sentence on both of you for the murder of the Duchess Ludmila. No longer will I tolerate the injustice of your crime in my realm. In accordance with the laws of Bohemia, I sentence you to be hanged by the neck until you are dead. May God have mercy on your souls."

Tunna and Gommon lost their arrogance in a moment. Dragomíra's face went white, and Boleslav look startled. I was sure they never dreamt that Václav could be so decisive.

Žito began to carry out our lord's orders, but the other guards hesitated.

"Now, Your Grace?" one of them asked.

Václav nodded. "Now. The sentence is to be carried out immediately so all may know that I will not hesitate to punish the guilty, especially those who have no regard for the lives of the innocent."

As the condemned were marched out of the hall, Václav turned his determined gaze on his mother and brother.

"I suppose we are next?" Boleslav said, frowning.

"Why? Have you committed sacrilege or murder, my brother?" Although the words were scornful, I heard the sorrow in my master's voice. When Boleslav did not answer, Václav turned to Dragomíra.

"I have a duty to God to honor you as my mother, but you have dishonored the office of regent and brought reproach upon our country with your unjust actions. Your policies have persecuted many innocent people and ended the lives of many Christians. I cannot let that go without consequence."

Dragomíra swallowed, but she said nothing in her defense.

"Therefore, I banish you from Bohemia so your destructive influence will never again poison our lands. You may return to Stodor, the land of your birth, but I want you to leave tonight. An escort will take you to the northern border." Václav folded his trembling hands and took a deep breath. His mother dropped her head in resignation. She knelt in her place.

"You are lenient, my lord." She remained on her knees until the guard helped her stand.

"As for you, Boleslav," Vaclav said, "I cannot let you go with our mother, nor can I let you leave Bohemia, at least not until I have married and produced a legal heir. Therefore, I will confine you to Castle Stara, where you shall live until further notice."

Boleslav's jaw dropped. It appeared that he would explode with anger. Before he could shout, however, Žito whipped out a cloth and gagged him with it. The other guard bound the resisting prince's hands, and they led him out, with Dragomíra following.

Václav sighed and looked at the silent *voyvodes* and stunned soldiers.

"One thing more," he said. "I know there are many in this room who feel Bohemia must fight all opposition, and that our sovereignty and independence are the most important things.

"But I tell you that there are times when choosing not to fight is the bravest course of action. You know I have fought the Duke of Bavaria and stand ready to fight the Magyars who killed my father, should they again threaten our borders." The men were hanging on his every word.

"Now the Germanic king, Henry the Fowler of Saxony, is poised to invade Bohemia. Fight him, you may say: fight and die. But die you surely would! We would all die, and Bohemia would be completely under the Fowler's control. There would be no more Čechs in the land.

"As Duke of Bohemia and Prince of all the Čechs, my decision is to meet Henry alone and negotiate with him."

The assembled men began to murmur then, but Václav held up a hand to silence them.

"Hear me, loyal Čechs. In battle we cannot defeat the Fowler's vast army. But we can defeat his intentions to subjugate us if we remain strong. A unified nation of Čechs will survive, and cannot be destroyed."

Ladislav, the eldest among the *voyvodes*, stepped forward and raised his fist. "I would rather die fighting than to live a coward under Saxon rule!"

The others joined in, making a clamor.

"All right!" Václav shouted, jumping to his feet. "All right. Then we will fight Henry and his powerful army! We will all die needless deaths. I am ready to meet my God, so it will not distress me to die.

"And Ladislav, I will tell your wife and daughters to ready themselves for the coming of the Saxons. They should know that the soldiers will first violate them, and then they will rip their bellies open and spill their entrails on the ground."

He pointed to the others. "And I will tell all your wives and mothers and daughters the same. Your young children will become sport for the Saxon soldiers or, if they are lucky, merely their slaves. Is that really what you want?"

His words echoed into a silence so profound that I could hear my heart beating. Ladislav's anger began to drain away. He stood facing my master for several minutes. At first I feared he would continue to defy his duke, but finally he went down on one knee and pulled his sword from its sheath. Grasping the point in his gloved hand, he handed it hilt first to Václav.

"I am your man, Your Grace."

My master raised him up. "God bless you, loyal Ladislav," he said. "You served my father faithfully, and I know you love Bohemia."

One by one the other *voyvodes* paid Václav homage. I saw the glimmer of tears in his eyes as he received each of them. Finally he dismissed the assembly.

"If I do not return, you must ready the castle's defenses. I pray that the Fowler is a man of honor." He grinned at the *voyvodes*. "Even if he is a Saxon."

Chapter 14

LESS THAN AN hour later, three of us rode out from the castle. I struggled to hold Václav's banner upright through a loop on the saddle as he and Žito cantered northwest along the road leading through the fields. I didn't dare tell my master I'd never ridden a horse before or he might not have let me come with him. Also unknown to my master, my tunic bulged with apples and other tidbits in case I needed to protect the three of us by appeasing the spirits of the trees and ponds and streams along our way. I worried that he would not approve of the traditional offerings.

Václav slowed our pace only when we reached the edge of the forest. Since the path wound along the outskirts of the dark, brooding trees, my master did not push us.

While our horses walked I did not have to concentrate so intently on the banner or on holding my mount with my knees. Instead, I pondered the doubts that had nagged at me ever since the audience in the great hall.

How could my master have been so merciful to Dragomíra and Boleslav? Surely he knew that they would never change. Didn't he realize the risks he was taking by letting them live—risk not only to his own life but to his dreams for Bohemia?

Fortunately, I did not have to put my thoughts into words. Žito was already voicing the same concerns.

"My lord," he said, frowning, "forgive me, but don't you see how dangerous it is to let Prince Boleslav and the duchess live? They will never yield to your authority, and they will continue to inflame the pagans against you."

"Peace, Žito," said Václav as he shifted in his saddle and looked at the big man. "I understand your concern and am more grateful than you can know for your loyalty and devotion." He turned to me and added, "And yours, also, Poidevin.

"However," he continued, "I cannot and I will not put my mother and brother to the sword. Boleslav is the legal Přemyslid heir until I have one of my own. My mother was baptized and once claimed faith in Christ. Do I dare slay one of God's children? Should I not pray for his mercy instead?" Václav sighed, looking weary.

"I must not succumb to the temptation to rid myself of everyone who opposes me. That is what they did when they ordered the murder of my blessed grandmother. I will not send them to hell without the grace of confessing their sins." He shook his head to emphasize his decision. "I will leave them in God's hands."

"But, my lord, you had Tunna and Gommon executed," I pointed out.

"Yes, Poidevin, because they committed the murder. As duke, I have the terrible responsibility to carry out the laws of Bohemia."

I could not let it rest, though. "But, Master, aren't those who ordered the murder as guilty as the men who did the deed?"

Václav breathed deeply, letting patience settle over him like a mantle. "May I not be merciful where I am able? I pray to rule peacefully, as Joseph did in Egypt. I do not have the stomach to lead with force, the way the warrior Joshua did."

His argument silenced me. Though my fears for his safety were no less, I kept them to myself.

We managed our pace for the rest of the afternoon, pausing twice to water the horses. I offered an apple to the spirit of the pond when my master wasn't looking, but grew more careless at the stream. Seeing what I was doing, Václav gripped my wrist and startled me so that I dropped the apple into the water prematurely.

"Poidevin!" he said sternly. "What are you doing?"

I hung my head and whispered, "I just wanted to protect us, my lord."

He gripped my chin and lifted my head so I had to look into his dark eyes. My heart sank at the thought of having displeased or angered him. I could barely suppress a whimper.

"Poidevin," he repeated, more gently this time, "come with me."

Still gripping my wrist, we strode along the bank of the stream to an overgrown place nearby. When he stopped, Václav released my arm and pulled away the tangled brambles.

I gasped. There was a roughly carved image of one of the forest's many gods. My fingers itched to hold an apple so I might offer it to the spirit in exchange for protection from hidden evil. To my horror, my master gripped the wooden idol and strained to pull it loose from the earth where it had become imbedded over the years. Without a word Žito added his strength to the task. The two of them managed to break the idol free and send it tumbling into the stream with a mighty splash.

I stared first at the ripples in the stream, then at the damp hole where the image had been. Finally I looked into Václav's smoldering eyes. Knowing I was an unworthy servant, both to my master and to his God, I fell to my knees and covered my head in shame.

"I'm sorry, my lord," I wailed. "Please, forgive me. I am afraid that evil will overcome us."

Václav raised me up and gripped my shoulders. His anger had turned to sorrow. "I know that old habits and superstitions are difficult to break, but these pagan gods are false. It is wrong to make sacrifices to them." His voice grew quiet. "But I need say no more, Poidevin. I forgive you, but I ask that if you pray, you pray only to the one true and living God from this day forward."

I nodded. "I will, Master." It was an easy promise to make; I never wanted to see that disappointed look directed at me again.

He smiled grimly. "Good." Then my master turned to Žito.

"We've rested long enough," said Václav, as if nothing had happened. "We'd best be on our way."

We mounted our horses and continued on our journey. I tried not to drown in self-pity while I contemplated my foolishness. I knew better! Václav himself had taught me! And while my horse plodded along behind the others, I prayed to the one true God for the courage to grow in faith and wisdom. Only then would I truly become worthy of my master.

The sun hovered close to the horizon and our shadows stretched out far beside us when we crested a hill and looked down upon a vast army. I did not know there were so many men in all the world. Václav halted his horse. I could only stare in amazement at the scene in the valley below. Warriors swarmed like ants, settling horses, pitching tents, and setting up camp for the night. Pikes bristled like a forest of bare branches. Sunlight gleamed off the metal points.

I remembered our proud army riding out, led by Václav, to fight against the Duke of Bavaria. It had seemed such a great number, but it had not been even half the number of men I saw now. I trembled in fear.

"Raise the flag of truce, Žito," my master said.

Žito pulled a white cloth from his saddlebag and tied it below the head of his lance. Václav held out his hand, and Žito passed the lance to him.

"I will go alone. You and Poidevin wait here for me." When Václav turned toward the army I cried, "No!"

He looked back at me, and I reddened. "I'm sorry, my lord," I said.

"I am not sorry," growled Žito. "We have come this far, my lord, and we should go with you. The Fowler would only become suspicious should you go alone."

Václav looked at us both. Finally he nodded. "You may come, then."

I let out the breath I'd been holding. Žito and I followed behind our master and on either side of him. All the while we drew nearer, my legs quivered against my horse. I knew we could not guard our master from this horde of well-armed Saxons.

The soldiers parted for us but clustered close by, staring. I tried to ignore them and focus on my master's proud stature, but the murmuring, bearded men-at-arms in their grimy leathers set my teeth chattering.

Václav led us to the heart of the army encampment where the largest pavilion had been erected. It had to be the king's tent, because a score of guards drew their swords as we approached.

One of them shouted at us in guttural tones. Though I did not understand the German language, it appeared that my master did. He replied in kind, and the man strode back to the pavilion's entrance.

In a moment another man came out, and I could only suppose that this was Saxony's king, Henry the Fowler. He held himself regally, his conical helm rimmed by a gold circlet. Though he wore chain mail and leathers like his men, a mantle of rich fabric was fastened at the king's shoulder with a gold brooch.

Before King Henry spoke or moved any closer to us, the soldiers indicated that the three of us should dismount. Žito and I marched behind Václav as we had ridden, still holding our respective banners. The soldiers allowed us to approach the king, but not too closely. We were once again halted by pikes thrust into our path.

Then my master went down on one knee and slowly pulled his sword from its scabbard. The pike men beside him grew wary, but Václav reversed the blade and offered it hilt first to the opposing king.

I did not understand what my master told King Henry in German, but it seemed to satisfy the older man. He stepped forward and took the sword by the hilt, nodding that Václav should rise. He glanced first at me, then longer at Žito with the most piercing blue eyes I had ever seen. At last Henry the Fowler beckoned for Václav to enter the great pavilion with him.

Chapter 15

ŽITO AND I stood outside until after darkness fell. Soldiers came and went all around us, most staring, some attempting to speak with us, but always there were at least two who had their weapons trained on us. Campfires blazed in the night. Soon the scent of roasting venison wafted on the air, making my mouth water. I dared not even glance at Žito, much less speak to him. My arms ached from holding Václav's banner for so long.

Just as it seemed the banner would fall from my numb hands, the door flap of the king's pavilion opened. My master and the Fowler stepped out; both were smiling. Václav said something in German, and Henry roared with laughter.

What charm did my master have that even an enemy Saxon king could be at ease with him in such a short time?

I could tell Žito desperately wanted to ask our duke what had happened, but he stood as still as stone and waited for Václav and King Henry to finish their conversation. I glanced around at the Germanic soldiers. They seemed as puzzled as Žito and I were. After all, wasn't this an army on its way to destroy Bohemia?

Finally my master bowed to the king, and the Fowler returned to his tent.

"We are to be given our own tent for the night," Václav said, as if that were not a miracle. "In the morning, King Henry and an honor guard of fifty warriors will ride back to Praha with us."

"Why, my lord?" Žito asked.

"I made a treaty with the Fowler, and he wants to come and personally see Praha before I pay him tribute."

"Tribute?" Žito grumbled. "A ransom to foreigners, isn't that what you mean?"

Václav smiled at the murmuring soldiers nearby. "Peace, Žito, and come with me to our tent where I will explain further. Do not raise your voice again."

We followed our escort to a hastily erected tent not far from the Fowler's pavilion. Once inside, we made ourselves comfortable and waited for the duke's explanation.

"I realize my decision will not be welcomed by every Čech," Václav said in a hushed voice. "I believe it necessary, however, and someday you will realize it was the only decision I could have made for Bohemia."

"But, my lord, to pay tribute to Saxony!" Žito said. "Does that mean King Henry is now our overlord?"

"Technically, I suppose it may," Václav said. "Bohemia, however, will remain independent of Saxony's laws. We are a sovereign country, Žito, and will remain so."

"It goes against all my Čech pride, my lord, to submit to the Saxons." Žito frowned.

"I understand." Václav gripped his shoulder. "But we must not allow our love for Bohemia to govern our good sense. The Fowler's army is far mightier than ours and could easily crush all opposition. By paying a yearly tribute, we will save Bohemia, and also gain the king of Saxony as our ally. United, we can stand against the Magyars. Perhaps we will finally be able to beat those invaders back from our borders."

Václav's explanation made perfect sense. Still, Žito still did not look happy. I supposed it was partly his nature and partly the nature of his position as the duke's bodyguard to be suspicious of everyone.

"How do you know, my lord, that the Fowler will uphold this agreement?" Žito asked.

Václav shrugged. "I can only pray he is a man of his word, as he seems to be."

"I fear you are far too trusting, my lord." Žito crossed his arms across his broad chest.

My master nodded. "You are probably right, my friend. But when I cannot trust anyone else I will always trust in God. My trust in him has never been betrayed. People—even mothers and brothers—are not always true to their word. But I have accepted this solution by faith—faith in God first and only then in the Saxon king's integrity."

I had a nagging doubt inside, remembering how Boleslav had tried to marshal the people against my master by stirring up Čech pride. I thought Václav must have noticed this.

"What troubles you, Poidevin?" he asked.

"Čechs have always been proud, my lord," I said. "Won't your decision anger some of the *voyvodes*? Won't Boleslav say that you cowered before the enemy and sold Bohemia to the Fowler?"

Václav sighed. "There is nothing I can say or do that will change my brother's views. I can only pray that God's grace will guide Boleslav to realize his grievous errors before it is too late. That is why I must allow him and the duchess to complete their days—to give them time to see the truth and repent.

"We are a proud people, Poidevin. But pride is a dangerous thing. Too little, and we become lazy and irresponsible. Too much, and we destroy ourselves." Conviction illuminated his eyes. "I must do what I believe in my heart will be best for all Čechs, whether or not they believe it, too."

With that, the conversation ended. Later, I tried to focus on the words of my master's evening prayer rather than the growing fear in my heart. I suspected even then that Bohemia was not ready for Václav.

Chapter 16

*V*ÁCLAV SENT ŽITO ahead to start the preparations necessary for the visiting king. By the time we returned to Praha with the Fowler and his guard of fifty men, the castle inhabitants had mobilized and the feast was ready. I went to assist in the kitchen, while Žito and his loyal guards attended my master.

All the *voyvodes* had remained in Praha to see what would become of their duke. Kitchen gossip revealed that while some resented the treaty with the Saxons, others were relieved not to fight them. It was not the unified Bohemia Václav had hoped to achieve.

After the steward seated the Fowler beside my master at the head table, I poured wine into their goblets.

Václav and King Henry conversed throughout the meal. Because they spoke in German, however, I did not know what they were saying. The Saxons on the Fowler's right seemed subdued. Likewise, the *voyvodes* to my master's left sat like stones, staring alternately at the king or his men.

My eyes roamed from face to face among the Čechs. Most I recognized, but a few had not been present during Dragomíra's regency. Probably they had not been welcome. Father Pavel and Father Balád were among the many priests, and some of the *voyvodes* had brought their wives and daughters with them.

At last I saw Přibislava sitting with her friend Ana. They were giggling behind their hands when Ana's father, Žibrid, a gruff-looking man with shaggy black brows, scolded them. I thought Ana turned to look at me, but I realized with a start that she was watching Václav. The girl blushed with embarrassment.

Knowing that my master would notice her, I wished I could veil her or send her away. He was now the duke. Everyone expected him to marry and produce a son to carry on the Přemyslid dynasty. He would not want to leave the country in the hands of Boleslav.

My feelings were mixed and my thoughts confused. I knew that Ana was kind, generous, and devout to the Most High God. She was everything that would matter to Václav when he chose a wife. But I feared that when he married I would lose my place beside him. When Václav had a son of his own, it would be unlikely that he would ever call me "son" again. If I could no longer serve him, I might as well be sacrificed to Morana, after all.

None of my fears, however, were realized that night. Though the feast went on for hours; though the kitchen boys brought platter after platter of meats, cheeses, breads, and sweets; though the musicians never stopped playing, my master never noticed Přibislava's friend. This was Henry the Fowler's feast, and Václav made sure the king stayed at the center of everyone's thoughts.

I tried to forget about Přibislava and her honey-haired friend and watch the faces of the *voyvodes* instead. I knew my master would want to know which of them appeared resigned and which still seemed hostile to his actions. But every time I glanced toward the two girls, Ana was either gazing dreamily at Václav or giggling with his sister.

The next morning Václav held a formal court in the great hall. He wore his crown and ducal robe. King Henry sat beside him wearing a golden circlet and cradling his scepter. Žito and Father Pavel took their places beside Duke Václav.

I stood nearby, where I could scan the faces of nearly everyone in the hall. Half were the Fowler's men, and half were our *voyvodes* and Václav's loyal soldiers.

Two of Václav's guard carried a wooden chest through the crowd and set it at his feet, bowing low before they backed away. Václav stepped down from his chair and turned to King Henry.

"My lord," he said, speaking first in German and then in Čech, "In exchange for the friendship of Saxony and your mighty protection of Bohemia, here are five hundred pieces of silver, which I pledge to you as a yearly tribute from Bohemia. In addition, one hundred twenty oxen are outside waiting to be taken to your army."

While my master presented the tribute to our new overlord, I watched the *voyvodes*. I tried to remember the names of the discontented nobles. Fortunately Žito was also watching them. Some looked on the scene thoughtfully, but others could not hide their anger or dismay. I did note that every one of the grim faces belonged to a *voyvode* who still clung to the old religion. I was grateful that Boleslav was not present.

As soon as Václav dismissed the assembly, the Fowler and his men left the castle. They returned to their army with the five hundred pieces of silver and the oxen. Though most of the Čechs were at least resigned to Václav's solution and grateful for Henry's protection from the Magyars, the pagan *voyvodes* smoldered with resentment.

I supposed there would always be opposition to my master's decisions. I remembered the story Václav had read to me about the man Noah and a great flood. At that time the whole world had turned against the Most High God. Only Noah and his family remained faithful. Sometimes it seemed that very few men were truly loyal to my master. Many, however, pretended to be so with professions of empty words.

To quietly celebrate his avoidance of war with Saxony, my master asked his most trusted inner circle to dine with him the following evening. This inner circle included the *voyvodes* who had supported him from the beginning, one of whom was Ana's father, Žibrid. Also present were Fathers Pavel and Balád, along with other priests I had not met. Přibislava, of course, was there with her friend, though they sat apart with the other daughters and wives.

"I want you to know how much I appreciate each of you and your faithfulness to Bohemia and to me," Václav began. He waited until I refilled his goblet before lifting it in toast. The men murmured their agreement and drank also.

"I believe with all my heart that God has delivered us from our enemies," he continued, "enemies both within the realm and outside her borders. I want all of you to know that I plan to rebuild the churches and recall all the banished priests. If need be, I will ask the bishop of Ratisbon to send us more priests to serve the people."

"Your Grace," asked the older Ladislav, his brows furrowed, "are you saying that you mean to bring Germanic priests into Bohemia?"

"Pardon me, Your Grace," asked Žibrid, who was as dark as his daughter was fair, "but paying tribute to the Fowler is unpopular enough. I would caution you about bringing in their priests as well."

Václav calmly set his goblet on the table. "Faithful *voyvodes*," he said, "I understand your reluctance to deal with Saxony. But in order to avoid the destruction of the Čech people and preserve Bohemia so she is her own master, I had no choice but to pledge my fealty to King Henry."

"Yes, yes, my lord," Ladislav said impatiently, "I do not approve, but I am beginning to understand. What I do not understand is the need for foreign priests."

Václav held up a hand to forestall further protests. "The churches must be rebuilt, but because of Dragomíra's policies, we don't have enough priests from among our own people. I will ask King Henry for priests to help us, but there will be one condition."

"What is that, my lord?" Žibrid asked.

My master folded his hands. "If they do not already speak the language of the Čechs, they will be required to learn it."

Žibrid inclined his dark head. "So, Your Grace," he said, "this is your plan? To conquer the Saxons one priest at a time?"

Many laughed at that, and the tense mood melted away.

Chapter 17

ONCE MY MASTER took the power from Dragomíra and Boleslav, I expected that our late-night sessions would come to an end. After all, Duke Václav had a kingdom to rule and more important things to consider than the education of a servant. Yes, I had accompanied him and Žito to meet with the Fowler. Yes, he had requested that I be his personal servant and take up residence in the tower with him and Žito. But somehow I did not think that this would include further lessons, especially since I had already learned how to read.

One day Václav and I were silently poring over a passage in the Psalms describing God's creation when a question I had wanted to ask for some time escaped my lips.

"Master, how do we know that our God is real?"

Václav's eyes blazed with fervor. The intensity of his gaze compelled me to want to understand. After a few moments, he spoke.

"Do you remember the storm last summer? The one with torrential rain that caused the river to overflow its banks?"

I nodded. "Yes, my lord."

He smiled. "And do you remember the lightning, the thunder, and the strong winds?"

"Yes, my lord." Ashamed, I also remembered my terror. I had cowered under a table, listening to the howl of the raging wind.

"Did you see the wind, Poidevin?"

I nodded and then frowned in puzzlement. "I suppose not, my lord. But I saw the roofs blown off the cottages and large trees pulled out by their roots."

Václav's eyes grew merry. "You saw the evidence of something invisible, evidence of something with great power. It is the same with God, though his power is far greater than even the most powerful windstorm."

My frown deepened. "So God is greater than the wind because he made the wind?"

"Yes," said Václav. "God made the sun, the moon, the stars, the forests, the mountains, and every creature that lives and breathes. But there is more."

Understanding dawned, much like the first rays of sunlight peering over the castle wall each morning. "Because God made everything, we must worship him only and no other gods?" I asked the question because I was not certain I had spoken it correctly.

"Yes!" Václav shouted, gripping my shoulder. Then he laughed, a joyous sound.

His delight was contagious. I grinned, well-pleased that I had finally grasped a small part of the truth that my master had so patiently taught me.

⁂

Without Dragomíra and her younger son to worry about, I found a new distraction over the next peaceful months.

I knew it was inevitable that my master would notice Ana eventually. The manner of their meeting, however, caught me by surprise.

I accompanied Václav to St. George's Basilica, to help him carry sacks of grapes. My master took great satisfaction in presenting the best grapes from his vineyard for making the wine that would be used by the priests at Mass.

"After all," he said, "even King David did not want to make an offering to God that cost him nothing. A greater gift is a purer sacrifice."

When we entered the quiet nave, first I thought the church was empty. There was no sign of a priest. We approached the altar bearing our offering. Our footsteps sounded hollow as they echoed.

Because my eyes were focused on the altar, I did not see the veiled figure kneeling at the rail until we were almost upon her. When she turned, I glimpsed a honey-colored braid beneath the dark veil.

"Forgive me for intruding on your prayers, my lady," my master whispered. Then he and I left the grapes at the altar and turned to go.

I wanted to hurry him to the door, but he walked slower than I'd ever seen him, stealing glances until we stepped outside.

"Who is she?" he asked me, turning back with a thoughtful expression. "I've seen her before."

I swallowed before a lie could escape my lips. I had never lied to him before, and I wasn't going to begin then.

"She is," I stammered, "Přibislava's friend."

"Oh, yes," Václav said. "The daughter of Žibrid?"

I nodded, hoping the conversation would end there.

"Do you know her name?" His eyes meeting mine showed compassion for my unease.

My throat tightened. I had to force out the word. "Ana, my lord."

"Ana," Václav whispered the name as if it were a prayer. Hearing him speak her name like that drove a spike through my heart.

Just as we started to leave, the door opened behind us and Ana stepped out. She seemed startled to see us there. With a glance at me, she dipped in a curtsy.

"Your Grace," she said, her eyes lowered.

"My Lady Ana."

As she rose, the girl lifted her eyes and smiled. The effect was staggering to me. How much more must it have been to my master?

"Your Grace knows my name?" she asked.

"Well, my lady," Václav said, and I could tell he was embarrassed, "I have just learned it from Poidevin here."

Ana turned her gaze on me. I felt both pleased and angry—pleased that she would look at me, and angry that she was being so coy with my master.

"Poidevin is very faithful." I wasn't sure what she meant by that.

"Yes, my lady," Václav said, pausing. I'd never seen him at a loss for words before. "Do you often come to St. George's to pray?"

She pushed a stray hair from her eyes. "I try to come at least twice in the week, my lord."

Václav glanced at me. "I am making plans to build a church within the castle walls, devoted to Saint Vitus." He swallowed. "It will take some time, but you are welcome to pray in my chapel if something prevents you from coming here."

Ana's eyes shone, but I didn't think it was because of Václav's chapel. "Your chapel? Where would that be, Your Grace?"

"In the castle, in my . . . my tower," he stammered, and his face appeared to flush. "Of course, if you would send me word, I can make sure you are left undisturbed. My man Žito will make sure of it."

"Žito? Is that your fearsome guard?"

Why, I thought, *oh why did she have to look so appealing?*

"Fearsome? I suppose so," Václav said with a shrug. "He is gruff only because it is his duty to keep me safe. Of course, he would not have to worry about keeping me safe from you."

While we accompanied Lady Ana back to the castle, I could only think how my master seemed to disregard his own safety. And while he and the girl talked and laughed together, forgetting my presence, my uncharitable suspicions about her grew. They were not based on anything untoward that she had said or done, but solely on my jealousy. I feared that Ana was about to steal precious time from me, time that I had hoped to spend in service to Duke Václav. My vague dreams of becoming something more to him, a soldier or a bodyguard, evaporated like the morning mist under the midday sun. How was it that a giggling girl could acquire such a stranglehold on my future?

Chapter 18

"MY LORD!" Žito called out early one morning. My master was just kneeling to say his prayers.

"Peace, Žito," Václav said, holding up a hand to prevent the guard from speaking. "I am sure your message is important, but my appointment with God is even more so. Come and pray with Poidevin and me, and then I'll hear your message."

"But, my lord! This is urgent . . ."

Václav silenced him with a look and bowed his head again.

Žito grumbled but did not try to argue further. I stifled a laugh at the sight of the burly warrior meekly kneeling beside me.

After a few minutes of silence, in which I asked for wisdom (Václav had taught me it was proper to ask for this), the three of us silently rose and went back to the bedchamber. Žito delivered his message.

"A duke of Moravia, Radslav of Kourím, claims to be 'the true Prince of the Čechs' because he advocates war with Saxony rather than submitting to the Fowler's tribute," Žito said, barely reining in his anger. "My scouts report that he is gathering an army. He intends to attack Praha, kill you, and proclaim himself Duke of Bohemia."

Václav appeared unconcerned while I fastened the many ties on his formal robe. "I have heard of this Radslav of Kourím," my master replied calmly. "My father fought with him in one of the battles against the Magyars. He judged him a valiant warrior, although lacking good sense, especially where the lives of others are concerned."

"But, my lord, he is raising an army!" Žito said.

My master paused. "It's a pity that ruined Moravia has brought Radslav to this folly. If it is true that the Duke of Kourím marshals an army against me, then I fear many will suffer for his foolishness." He turned to me and waited while I settled the gold coronet on his brow. "I will pray for wisdom in this matter."

I couldn't help but smile, and Václav raised his brows in question. "What is it, Poidevin?"

I shrugged. "I just thought it curious, my lord, how I have been asking God for wisdom this morning at the same time you are searching for it."

My master nodded. There was a twinkle in his eye. "Thank you, Poidevin. Once again you have anticipated my needs." Then he turned to his bodyguard.

"Come, Žito, break your fast with us. This morning we will be joined by many peasants from the Moravian frontier. They have come to ask for our help. Now I understand why they need it. Perhaps some of them will have more information about Duke Radslav and his plans."

Žito followed with a grim expression.

Our meal of cheese and black bread was shared with a group of haggard-looking families, refugees from the border area. Václav greeted the peasants as if they were as important to him as King Henry the Fowler. After he exhorted them to work hard and be of good cheer, he asked God's blessing on the meal. The poor wretches, especially the children, gobbled their food and were eager for more. Václav let them eat their fill and directed servants to take the women and children to the kitchen and provision them for their continuing journey.

He turned to the men and began to ask them questions about the duke and his army.

"They burned us out, Your Grace," said a man with dark circles under his eyes. "Duke Radslav said that anyone who refused to bow the knee to him would be hanged."

Václav looked thoughtful. I could tell he was more worried about the innocent people and their suffering than he was about any threat to him personally.

He stood and his gaze met Žito's. In his embroidered robe and gold coronet, Václav looked like an avenging angel.

"Inform the guard that this morning's court is canceled. Have the battle commanders meet me in the tower as soon as possible."

Žito stepped forward and bowed. "As you will, my lord." As he strode from the hall, Václav turned to me.

"Come, Poidevin. We have an army to prepare."

I held my head high as I followed him, feeling the eyes of the displaced villagers upon us. It was difficult not to feel superior to them as we passed by, but I tried to remember what my master said about pride and its inevitable fall. After all, it had not been so long ago that I was a wretched orphan in rags.

Early the following morning, I rode beside Václav and Žito at the head of a small army, all those who could be called on short notice. We headed east, toward the Moravian border where Duke Radslav and his men had last been seen. My master felt it would be best to show our resolve by meeting them head-on, rather than waiting for them inside the castle.

Each time we stopped to water the horses or camp for the night, I felt a twinge of fear about not offering to the spirits of the forest. But I recalled my master's words, how the gods of the old religion were not true gods and not even worthy of notice. I hoped that as my faith in the one true and living God increased, I could one day banish all my fears.

We caught our first glimpse of the enemy army on the third day out from Praha. Though they seemed a great multitude, in reality they did not have many more men than we did. When we stopped, Václav beckoned me to his side.

"I must pray alone now. Come and inform me when my things are unpacked."

"Yes, my lord." I took the reins of his horse and watched him go apart a little way and fall on his knees.

We camped across a wide valley from Duke Radslav's army that evening. As soon as the soldiers finished erecting Vaclav's tent, I approached him. When he did not notice my footsteps, I cleared my throat before interrupting his prayer.

"My lord, all is ready."

He opened his eyes and stood. After we reached his tent, he directed me to take out his writing implements.

"What do you wish to write, my lord?" I laid out ink, quill, and parchment on a camp table.

"I'm sending a message to Duke Radslav," he said as he dipped the quill in the ink.

I leaned as close to the table as I dared, trying to read Václav's careful script, but looking upside down I could only decipher a few words, and they meant nothing to me. The message was not long, and by the time my master signed his name at the bottom, the ink near the top was almost dry. I brought him the box with the ducal seal. He blew on the parchment, folded it, dripped hot wax onto it, and pressed the heavy ring with the flaming eagle emblem onto the wax.

"Here." He handed me the message. I was careful not to touch the still warm seal. "Take this to Žito and have him send a messenger to Duke Radslav's camp."

"Yes, my lord." I bowed and hurried from the tent, almost colliding with Žito.

"Here," I said, giving him the parchment. "Our master wishes you to make sure this gets to Duke Radslav."

Without a word, Žito headed toward the horses. I knew he would deliver the message himself. He trusted no one where Václav was concerned.

As I opened the tent to return to my master, I realized that Žito had not questioned me about the message. If I'd had any doubts about where I stood in Žito's estimation before, I could rest them now. He trusted me.

We did not have long to wait before Žito returned with Radslav's answer. The message had been a challenge from Václav to meet this Duke of Moravia in single combat. Radslav had accepted.

Zito's eyes narrowed to slits. "You cannot do this, my lord," he said. "I do not trust this pretender to fight fairly."

Václav looked up from Radslav's reply. "He has agreed to my terms: no interference from either side. If I win, his army returns to Moravia. It's the only way to prevent great loss of life on both sides."

Žito did not voice the obvious question: What would happen if Václav did not win?

Chapter 19

HE NEXT MORNING, I rode beside my master through the cheering ranks of his soldiers. He lifted a gauntleted hand in salute, though behind the conical helm his face was solemn.

I did not doubt Václav's prowess as a warrior. I had watched him often enough in the practice yard. He was equally skilled with sword, ax, mace, and bow. But Duke Radslav brought with him the force of wicked ambition, and, like Žito, I did not trust him to meet my master in fair combat.

At last we reached the valley. The appointed time had come. The entire Bohemian army lined up along our side of the grassy rise. The soldiers did all they could to present themselves as a formidable foe. Václav dismounted and handed me the reins.

"I wish that I could go with you, my lord," I said.

Though his face was set in determination, the light of hope still shone there. "And I wish that you could as well, Poidevin."

Accepting a wooden shield and battle-ax from a somber Žito, Václav strode toward the center of the empty valley. He carried himself like the noble duke he was, but I knew he would be praying for God's help with every step he took.

Duke Radslav's army appeared at the crest of the hill on the opposite side. When they saw us, they began howling and beating upon their shields. Our soldiers returned the deafening cry.

A massive armed figure, a giant compared to my master, broke away from the enemy army and headed toward Václav. Duke Radslav carried a shield and battle-ax, the chosen weapon; a gaudy coronet on his helm gleamed in the bright morning sun. His shield, breastplate, and leathers were dyed in brilliant shades of red and gold. In his unadorned armor, Václav looked like a common soldier—like David going out to meet Goliath.

Radslav shouted something unintelligible and raised his battle-ax. Yelling, he ran toward Václav and swung the ax at my master's head. Václav held up his shield. Chips of wood flew as he blocked the blow. Before Radslav could recover, Václav brought his ax around and down, but Radslav held up his blade, and Václav's glanced off it with a clang.

They circled one another, exchanged blows, circled again. Roaring, Radslav hammered blows upon my master, battering his shield, but Václav never wavered in his defense. The giant circled again and attacked from a new quarter, but Václav stepped aside. While Radslav was off-balance, my master smashed his ax into his opponent's shield, breaking it in two.

The enemy duke flung the halves of the shield away and gripped his ax with both hands. Bellowing, he hurled himself at my master, raising the ax to deliver a decisive blow. But Václav dropped his shield and swung his ax to meet Radslav's attack. The force of the clash knocked Radslav's ax from his hands.

As Radslav looked up, the sun broke through the clouds and shone upon my master's helm. The reflected light blinded the vanquished duke, and he fell to his knees.

Some in Radslav's army moved forward, and Žito shouted for the archers to ready their bows. But, to my surprise, Václav dropped his ax and lifted Radslav up, giving him the kiss of peace. My master spoke with him for several minutes, gesturing. Radslav hung his head and, leaving behind his ax and broken shield, strode back to his waiting army, climbed upon his horse, and led his men away.

As if Žito had given an unspoken signal, we all rushed down into the valley to meet our victorious duke. Václav held up his hands to silence our questions.

"God has given us the victory," he shouted.

"But, Your Grace, you let him go," Žito protested. Others added their voices to his.

Václav waited for the soldiers to grow quiet again. "Duke Radslav has been humbled this day in the sight of all his army. He will trouble us no longer."

I prayed that my master was right. Between his own mother and brother, the Magyars, the Bavarians, and fractious pagan nobles, the last thing Duke Václav needed was another enemy.

Chapter 20

*T*HOUGH I KNEW our master had to be even more saddle-weary than we were, Václav insisted on holding court at the castle the following day. Žito and I attended him.

As the day grew long, the line of people grew longer. The rainy weather, which had begun on our return to Praha, did not keep the peasants from coming to air their grievances to my master. In truth, he seemed to welcome the opportunity to hear their stories.

One young family could not pay their taxes because a drought in the southern part of Bohemia had devastated both fields and livestock. Václav paid their tax for them and sent them home with bags of grain and three sheep.

An old widow's house had been burned to the ground by Duke Radslav's men a fortnight before. Václav sent some of his soldiers to help her rebuild.

A drunken soldier had broken into the house of a peasant from Praha, injuring both the man and his wife, and making a shambles of their hut. Václav ordered the soldier to do all the couple's menial chores for a month and repair whatever he had damaged.

At last a group of ragged men and women were brought forward. I shuddered when I saw that their feet and hands were shackled. The scar on my ankle throbbed in empathy. Although it was difficult to tell because of their filthy condition, it seemed that some of them were no older than my master. Others, however, were certainly older, even Bora's age. Leading them was a portly merchant wearing a red cape caught at the shoulder with a huge enameled brooch.

"Your Grace," said the herald. "May I present Charles the Stout from the city of Rome who comes to sell choice slaves from Croatia and Macedonia."

To my surprise, Václav asked, "How much does he want for all of them?"

The trader named a sum. Since I knew nothing about money, I did not know if it was a large amount or not.

My master sat in silence for a moment, measuring the trader. His gaze kept returning to the line of slaves. Finally he beckoned to me.

"Poidevin," he whispered so that only I could hear, "bring me ten pieces of gold from the small chest in my bedchamber."

I bowed and quickly exited out the side door. My feet flew all the way to my master's tower. I lifted the corner of the stag hunt tapestry and pried out the piece of false wood paneling that concealed my master's valuables. He had shown me this place shortly after his coronation, but I'd not had a reason to open it before. I lifted the lid of the small wooden chest and counted one shiny gold piece for each of my fingers. I twisted them tightly in a fold of my tunic, returned the chest to its hiding place, and replaced the paneling and tapestry.

Hurrying back to the great hall, I watched with interest as Václav sealed his bargain with the grumbling merchant. On his way to the door the man smirked, and I gasped. I had no more time to wonder about what may have transpired, for Václav stood, compelling my attention.

"Bring the blacksmith," Václav said to a serving boy. "Quick as you can." The startled boy ran from the hall, and Václav turned his gaze on the anxious slaves. How well I remembered that mingled fear and resignation! To my surprise, Václav spoke a few words in their language. It made me happy to see their frightened looks turn to relief.

"Poidevin," Václav said.

"Yes, my lord?"

"Run to the stables and bring Demetrios. He is Macedonian, I believe."

"Yes, my lord, he is." I grinned and hurried as quickly as my long legs could carry me. Once Demetrios understood the reason for the Duke's summons, the older man tried to match my pace.

As Demetrios and I entered the hall, the blacksmith was removing the shackles from the slaves' wrists and ankles. Kitchen workers carried two large basins of water and set them on the floor. Ana and Přibislava got up from their cushioned seats and bade me carry one of the chairs to the nearest water basin. Then Ana helped the oldest slave, the one who reminded me of Bora, to the chair. Ana smiled at the bewildered woman, helping her put her dirty, bleeding feet in the water. Then with her own hands and a cloth that a servant handed to her, Ana gently bathed the slave's feet.

Astonished, I turned to my master, who was speaking to Demetrios. "Please tell them they are slaves no longer," Václav said. "I have paid the price for their freedom."

When Demetrios relayed my master's words, the elderly woman started to cry, and the others stared at Václav in surprise that quickly turned to gratitude. Those standing in the water stepped out and, with dripping feet, prostrated themselves before my master. One sobbing young woman kissed the ground in front of him. The two young men still in shackles bowed where they stood with a rustling of chains. The blacksmith finished breaking the shackles with a resounding clang of his hammer, and the two men rushed forward and dropped to their knees before Václav.

I glanced around the hall at the few other witnesses to this unusual purchase, including two *voyvodes*, peasant petitioners, and servants. Their faces revealed surprise and also delight at the generosity of their duke.

Václav beckoned to one male and one female servant. "Show these people to the men's and women's quarters. Let them bathe and give them new clothing. They will dine in the hall tonight."

The servants bowed, and the now freed slaves gratefully followed them, glancing over their shoulders at my master until they could no longer see him. Václav gestured for Demetrios to accompany them.

"You shall be their voice," Václav said.

"Then we will go with the women," Přibislava told her brother with a smile. She grabbed Ana's hand and hurried out.

While Václav finished listening to the rest of his petitioners, my mind wandered back to my arrival at Praha. I realized how different my life would be now had Václav not bought my freedom. My heart swelled with gratitude, and I was suddenly ashamed of the jealousy I had felt toward Ana. She was kind as well as beautiful. How many noblewomen would humble themselves to comfort an old slave? There could be no better duchess for my master than Ana.

🐾

Later that evening Přibislava approached me as I helped set the head table.

"Poidevin," she said.

I turned and bowed to her, realizing with a start that I was taller than she was now.

"Would you seat me and Ana beside my brother tonight?"

I could not answer her at first. She and Ana were usually present, of course, but Přibislava was so unassuming that the two girls nearly always sat in an unobtrusive spot. "I expect the duke would be honored," I managed to say, "since he has no special guests tonight."

The girls did sit next to the duke, but I was wrong about there being no special guests. Everyone but Václav seemed surprised when all of the freed slaves, now washed and wearing clean clothes, were seated below the head table, in a place of honor.

"Brother," Přibislava said while I poured her wine, "that was a most noble thing you did today." She indicated the strangers waiting patiently for something to eat.

"Yes, Your Grace," Ana said. "You have saved ten lives."

Since Přibislava sat between the two, Václav had to lean forward to better see Ana.

"It galls me to see helpless people treated so ill," he said.

"I had a thought, my lord." Ana's nose wrinkled impishly. "Do you think word will spread that you pay handsomely for slaves? Perhaps other traders will come to Praha to gain similar treasures for themselves."

Václav sipped his wine. "Did you consider that a handsome payment? I thought it quite small for precious souls and would pay it and more again." He shrugged. "But I will consider bargaining lower if another trader brings slaves to Praha."

Chapter 21

THE REST OF the evening passed pleasantly for those in the hall. My master had asked Demetrios to announce that the freed slaves were welcome to live in Bohemia or to make their way home. Not surprisingly, all ten decided to stay in Praha. They embarrassed Václav by prostrating themselves before him and trying to kiss his hands or touch his royal robe as he was leaving the hall. He seemed quite glad to retire to his tower and say his evening prayers.

It took me awhile to fall asleep that night because all I could see in my mind's eye was Ana's obvious admiration for my master. When at last I slept, it seemed only minutes before I was awakened from my servant's pallet on the floor near Václav's high bed. I'd heard him speaking softly in the chapel, and so I padded across the freshly strewn rushes and peered into the nearly dark alcove. A single candle provided the barest illumination. There was my master on his knees, praying out loud.

Not wishing to disturb him, I was about to turn around and return to my pallet when he stopped and stood up, grabbing the altar rail as if he were in pain.

"Master?" I whispered.

He whirled to face me. Tears glistened on his cheeks. "Poidevin, you startled me."

I dropped to my knees. "Forgive me, my lord, but I heard you."

He stepped forward and lifted me up. "No, Poidevin, it is you who should forgive me for waking you." He sighed.

"Have you been wrestling angels again?" I asked.

"Not angels precisely. More likely my conscience."

I did not understand, and he must have seen that on my face, even in the dim light, for he asked me to sit with him at the table. After placing the candle between us, he sat down and folded his hands.

"Even though I am determined to rule our country well, there was a time when I'd hoped to devote myself to God through the church."

I nodded, remembering the conversation we had more than two years before. It seemed so long ago. So much had happened since then.

"Knowing I can best serve God by ruling Bohemia does not make the idea of fulfilling my dynastic duty an easy one." He stared at the candle.

Dynastic duty? I wasn't sure what he meant by that, but it sounded ominous.

"As you may have noticed, I have been trying in a somewhat bumbling way to get to know Lady Ana better."

Now I guessed what dynastic duty must mean—fathering a son to rule after him. I thought then that my fears were coming true. My master would no longer need me to serve him, and I would no longer have a purpose in this world.

"Žibrid, her father, is a powerful and loyal *voyvode*." Václav tapped his fingers on the table.

My heart sank within me.

"The lady is gentle and God-fearing, but she also has wit and intelligence. She seems to be all that I could want in a Duchess." He swallowed, and I forgot my own misgivings as he looked into my eyes. "I will do my duty. I cannot do otherwise if

I wish to keep Boleslav from ruling our land with cruelty and hatred. But, Poidevin, I still grieve the fact that I will never be a priest."

I wanted to say something encouraging to him, brother to brother, not forgetting the chasm of rank between us, but sharing in what he saw as loss. Václav's marriage would, after all, also be a loss for me.

He must have recognized my feelings, for he shook himself out of his melancholy and asked, "But what cloud is over you, good Poidevin? You seem to share my misgivings tonight."

I pulled the words from deep inside myself. "I commend the Lady Ana to Your Grace as a wife. She is most virtuous and fair." To my chagrin, my voice cracked on the final word. I swallowed and said no more.

"But I suspect there is more here, Poidevin, and you must tell me." His eyes commanded me to answer him.

"I respect Ana as I do Přibislava." I swallowed to loosen the tightness in my throat. "But though you are my duke and my master, you have also been like a father—or an elder brother—to me. I have no other family, my lord. When you marry, I shall be alone in this world once again, and that frightens me." There, the words were out for both of us to see.

Václav covered his mouth with his hand, and I could tell that only his affection for me kept him from laughing out loud. "How little you know me if you believe that! *If* the lady will have me—"

"Oh, my lord, she will," I said, stopping when he held up a hand.

"If the lady will give me her hand in marriage, my affection for you will not lessen, Poidevin. Though you are my servant, we are brothers in adversity." He stood up. "Like the prophet

Daniel, we have faced all manner of lions: Dragomíra, Boleslav, King Henry, and now Duke Radslav."

I feared to say the words, but I had to know my fate. "But will you still need me to serve you after you marry?"

Václav brought his fist to his heart. "Faithful Poidevin, I will always need you by my side."

I went around the table and fell to my knees. As I had long ago, I put my hands between his and swore my fealty to him. Václav raised me up and gazed at me with a smile.

"Now that our hearts' burdens have lightened, it is time we slept. It will soon be morning," he said with a yawn. "But stay here until I reach my bed and then put out the candle."

"Yes, my lord," I said, feeling relief for the first time since Václav had begun to notice Ana.

While he climbed into his high bed, I turned and watched the candle's flame in the dark room. I'd never noticed before how much light a single candle could produce, how much darkness it dispelled. In that moment, a thought came to me. My master was like a flame burning brightly in the darkness of Bohemia, the darkness of selfishness, greed, ignorance, and an insatiable hunger for power. It was heartening to know how much goodwill one man could spread to others.

When I blew out the flame, however, the darkness instantly returned. I realized with a chill that Václav's flame could as easily be put out.

Chapter 22

*T*HE NEXT DAY, Duke Václav announced his decision to visit the northern districts of Bohemia, where Ana's father, Žibrid, lived. My master took Žito with him, but he asked me to stay at the castle to watch over Přibislava and Ana. This time, to my surprise, I felt needed rather than left out. After all, I alone knew why he was going and that it would not be long before he returned.

As soon as he and Žito left, Přibislava sent for me.

"What do you know, Poidevin?" she asked as she pulled me into her room. "Is Václav going to ask Ana's father for her hand in marriage?"

I opened and closed my mouth like a fish out of water. Václav had not said it was a secret, but neither had he given me permission to speak of it, even to Přibislava. "He did not say," I managed to squeeze out, though again my voice cracked on the final word.

"Poidevin!" Přibislava put her hands on her hips. "You are not speaking plainly with me. Did my brother say anything about Ana? Doesn't he like her at all?"

"Oh, yes," I said. "He likes her very well."

Přibislava grabbed my arms. "Then he *is* going to talk to her father. I know it!"

"If this were true, am I right in thinking it would please my lady?" I couldn't help but tease her.

"My dear fellow," she said, shaking me. "Don't you know me?"

I put on my most innocent face. "I have heard you say to Lady Ana that you always wanted a sister."

Přibislava shrieked. She grabbed my hand and pulled me through the castle and outside to the gardens. There we found Ana seated on a bench, staring at her hands. The brightness of her hair contrasted with the melancholy on her face.

"Ana!" Přibislava said breathlessly. "Here is Poidevin."

Ana stood, wringing her hands. The longing in her eyes made me ashamed that I had selfishly wished to keep her away from my master. I went down on one knee and faced her with a lightness of heart I had not felt before.

"Be of good cheer, Lady Ana," I said. "I can assure you that you have captured my master's heart."

Her eyes widened and her cheeks flushed. "Poidevin," she whispered, "don't toy with me. Are you telling me the truth?"

I was sure now that Ana would make an excellent wife for my master. She deserved my wholehearted devotion. "There is no doubt, my lady."

She closed her eyes and clasped her hands, breathing a silent prayer.

"What did I tell you?" Přibislava said. She seemed as pleased as if she had arranged the match herself. I could understand her feeling.

Ana looked at me shyly. "You know, Poidevin, I did not like you at first, because of all the time you spent with Duke Václav. I was jealous of you," she admitted. "He treats you more like a brother than a servant."

"And that is what Poidevin is," Přibislava said, winking at me.

Now it was my turn to be taken by surprise. Ana, jealous of a servant? Then both of us had been ridiculous.

When I thought about it, I realized that my master had room in his heart for many people: his beloved grandmother, Přibislava, Žito, Ana, even his wicked mother and brother. He was genuinely concerned for all the people of Bohemia. What Boleslav and others like him saw as Václav's weakness, I now understood was his greatest strength. Boleslav thought a duke should rule with an iron fist, crushing and bending others to his will like the bloodthirsty gods of the old religion. My master believed that a good ruler must balance justice with compassion. That came from his deep faith in a God of love.

Duke Václav had awakened a noble purpose within me, a desire to become like him and care for the needs of other people over my own. As I tried to live the way Václav did, I began to understand why he would not give up the hope that even his mother and brother would someday take up that noble purpose for themselves.

The last trace of my resentment for Ana vanished, and I silently pledged to serve her as faithfully as I served my master. I knew I could come to love her. Learning to love Dragomíra and Boleslav as Václav did? I doubted I could ever manage it.

Václav and Zito returned after nearly a fortnight with the good news that Žibrid had gladly granted his daughter's hand in marriage to my master. After the formal betrothal, Přibislava accompanied Ana back to her father's castle to prepare for the wedding. It would take place on the midwinter feast of Epiphany.

Since I no longer had my "bodyguard" duties, I pestered Žito about teaching me how to fight.

"Here," he said unexpectedly one day. "Try this." And with a smirk, Žito gave me a dagger of my own.

As I held the knife in my hand, I stared at it in awe. It was a plain blade, but sharp, and the hilt lay smooth in my hand. I could hardly wait to put the leather scabbard on my belt when Žito grabbed my other arm.

"What?" I said, startled. The way he looked me over reminded me of my first day at the castle, when the nobleman had examined my teeth.

"Since when has your tunic become so shabby?" he asked.

I shrugged. "I hadn't noticed."

"Come," said Žito, pulling me along. "You will disgrace our duke wearing clothes like these."

A short while later, I followed Žito to the great hall in order to serve our master. Though Žito walked on his feet, I walked on air, holding my head high. I was proud to be the personal servant of Duke Václav, and now I wore a new moss-green tunic with a shiny dagger in its scabbard on my belt. What more could I want?

Chapter 23

HEN THE WEATHER turned cold, I felt my old apprehension of the goddess Morana and the feast of winter solstice. Even though Boleslav could no longer threaten me, it was quite a shock when I discovered that Václav had invited his mother and brother to Praha for his wedding. Like the bride-to-be and Přibislava, they were to arrive in time for a new feast my master ordered to replace the pagan festival, a feast Bohemia had celebrated in years past, before Dragomíra's regency. As long as no sacrifices to Morana were planned, I could endure even Boleslav's presence for a fortnight.

As the feast day approached, I helped the servants festoon the castle with garlands of holly and evergreen branches. Cheery fires blazed brightly, but could not keep out all the cold. Dragomíra and Boleslav made their return to Praha just after a heavy snowfall and in less than a pleasant mood.

That first evening, Václav hosted a feast in the great hall to honor their return. Few *voyvodes* had arrived, since it was still several days before the wedding would take place. Dragomíra and Boleslav were outwardly cordial, but their hostility was apparent to me. The more Boleslav drank of the freely flowing wine, the more open his resentment toward his brother became.

When the time came to offer a toast, Václav stood up and started to speak. He was interrupted by a drunken Boleslav who came unsteadily to his feet and lifted his goblet.

"I drink to you, my brother and jailer. May your reign be short and your marriage unfruitful." He laughed, tossed back the dregs of his cup, and slammed it down on the table.

Not another sound could be heard in the hall. Václav stared at Boleslav for a long moment.

"I forgive you, brother, for your rudeness and ill wishes. It is the excess of wine that is speaking," he said.

"No," Boleslav interrupted him, "it is my heart that speaks to you now."

"Guards," said Václav, "take Prince Boleslav to his guest room and there let him seek sobriety."

"You have no right," Boleslav shouted while two heavyset guards dragged him out of the hall. The servants began to whisper among themselves.

Přibislava covered her face in embarrassment. Ana, sitting beside Václav, looked stricken.

"I apologize for my brother," Václav said to her. "You should not have had to hear that."

Just when it seemed the feast would be ruined, Father Pavel stood. "Your Grace, I would like to erase that curse with a blessing."

Relieved, my master inclined his head. "We would all be most grateful to you, Father."

The priest lifted both hands. "May the Lord bless your coming marriage. May he make you fruitful. May you both find joy in the Lord and in one another. In the name of the Father, and of the Son, and of the Holy Spirit. Amen."

Václav held out his hand to Ana, and she shyly stood up beside him. Goblets clanked around the tables as everyone stood and affirmed the priest's words.

Even though Dragomíra did not partake of the general goodwill, she managed to keep her peace. For that moment, I thought perhaps she had accepted the situation. But when she later excused herself, Žito pulled me to a corner of the hall.

"I need you to do a dangerous thing, Poidevin." He glanced around to make sure no one was listening.

My heart started pounding. "What is it?"

"I would do it myself, but I am easily recognized. I know you can make yourself invisible when you want to." He glared at me. "And I trust no one else where our master is concerned."

I nodded. At that moment I was willing to do anything for him. "What do you want me to do?"

"Shadow Dragomíra. See who she speaks with and listen to what is said. I suspect plots within plots." He gripped my arm. "If I could hide it from the duke, I would slit her throat and Boleslav's." He shook his head. "As long as those two live, our master's life is in jeopardy."

When I realized how much danger we might have to face in the days ahead, my knees felt like water. Duke Václav, Ana, Přibislava, Žito, and I were all at risk.

I delivered the remains of the feast to Bora and her husband later that night. As I was returning from their hut, I noticed two shadowy figures creeping toward the castle garden. My heart skipped a beat when I remembered Žito's words, and I slipped around the gate in order to approach unseen. I was able to get close enough to hear some of their whispered conversation.

"What do you think of Boleslav's chances to successfully overthrow his brother?" Dragomíra said.

A male voice that sounded like Ladislav's answered her. "Boleslav may now be of age, my lady, but the people love Václav.

We must be patient. The time is not yet ripe for him to over-throw his brother."

That traitor! I thought. *Pretending to be loyal to Václav.* I heard the rustle of fabric and realized they were heading in my direction. I crept away somewhat relieved that the danger to my master was not imminent, but terribly disturbed that one whom he thought was an ally had falsely sworn allegiance. Of course, knowing the duke, he would not want to confront Ladislav based only on an overheard conversation. After all, I had not seen the man's face, although I did know his voice. Žito and I would just have to keep a close watch on him. Maybe he would become overconfident and make a mistake that would reveal everything.

Chapter 24

THE NEXT DAY was Václav's new feast. He called it Christmas, a day honoring the birth of the son of the Most High God, Jesus Christ.

While I helped my master dress that morning, curiosity burned within me. "Master," I said, "since God has a son, then who is his mother? Is she a goddess?"

"No," he said with a chuckle. "The blessed Virgin Mary was a young girl."

Now I was hopelessly confused. I didn't even know enough to ask more questions. "The stories about the wise Joseph, the warrior Joshua, and Daniel in the lion's den are clear to me, my lord," I said. "But not this."

Václav gripped my shoulder. "The birth of Jesus Christ was a miracle. You will come to understand what it means in time, my son."

No one had ever seen a celebration like this one. Instead of important and honored guests, Václav had invited all the people of Praha to share it with him. Since they could not all fit in the great hall at one time, food was continually served from midday into the night. I divided my time helping in the kitchen and running back and forth between the kitchen and the hall. There was music and dancing along with the eating. My master, Ana, and Přibislava wore themselves out playing host to the steady stream of people, some wealthy, but most of them needy peasants.

Dragomíra and Ladislav were seated at the head table, watching Václav with distaste as he wrapped some food in a cloth for a crippled old man to take home with him. Fortunately, Boleslav was still restricted to his room. Otherwise, his sarcastic remarks about wasting good food on worthless peasants would never have ceased.

It was quite late when the last guest departed and Ana and Přibislava retired. Václav sat in a chair by the fire, watching the flames with a peaceful look on his face. I stood nearby, exhausted, but determined to guard his privacy. Since becoming duke, he had so few quiet moments.

Suddenly, Václav turned to me with a stricken look on his face.

"Poidevin, did Arnost the shepherd come to the feast today? I do not remember seeing him. His wife has a new baby."

I had seen Bora and many others that I knew from both the town and the nearby villages, but I could not remember seeing the shepherd's cheerful face or the limp he had from an old injury. "No, my lord," I answered at last. "Perhaps the weather is paining his leg."

My master stood up. "Gather what food you can carry, and I will get some firewood. We must bring Christmas to Arnost and his family."

"Now, my lord?" I glanced around at the bodies of servants asleep on the rushes. "The night is more than half over and outside is bitter cold, snow, and ice. What will Žito say?"

"Not to worry, Poidevin. You have surely stayed awake much later than this." His eyes twinkled. "And Žito has been sent on his own errand."

I hung my head. "Yes, my lord."

Václav cupped my chin in his gloved hand and lifted my head to face him. "Then meet me at the gate as soon as you have gathered the food and collected your cloak."

In less than half an hour, we were trudging through deep snow on a clear, frigid night. The stars sparkled as if made of jewels. The light of the moon showed us the way down the hill and past the sleeping city of Praha. The farther we walked, the deeper the cold penetrated my bones. I no longer felt the weight of the bag of provisions slung over my shoulder. Instead my body had turned numb.

I followed my master, watching the load of firewood strapped to his back. He seemed unaffected by the cold; his stride was steady through the knee-deep snow. At last I stumbled, falling into a bank of snow. I couldn't go on. The need for sleep overpowered me.

But Václav's strong hands lifted me up. He dusted the snow off my shoulders and handed the fallen sack to me. "Poidevin," he said firmly.

I forced my eyes open. My teeth were chattering so much I couldn't answer him.

"We must keep moving. Follow in my footsteps until we reach Arnost's cottage. It's not far now."

I nodded. Václav set off again, and I had to follow. Remembering his words, I tried to place my numb feet in each of my master's footprints. As we trudged on, each step became a little easier, and feeling began to return to my limbs.

Finally we reached a small hut nearly buried by a snow drift. No smoke rose from the chimney. It took a moment for me to realize just what that could mean.

"Hello!" my master called. There was no answer.

He pushed open the rickety door and we stepped inside. We were greeted by the smell and bleating of a few sheep. Only their warm bodies kept the hut from being as cold as the outside.

Someone groaned from a cot near the back wall.

"Arnost!" Václav exclaimed, dropping the wood. He knelt beside the cot and touched the man's forehead. "You're burning with fever."

"My wife took it first, Your Grace," the shepherd said in a raspy voice. "She and the baby are very weak, but I believe they will live if I can get some wood." Beside him stirred a woman. An infant's thin cry came from under the ragged blanket that covered the two adults.

"Poidevin, start a fire. We must help them."

I did so, and found a small pot in which to melt snow. Václav and I soon had the family sitting by a roaring fire, the man and his wife drinking strong herbs in a cup of hot water and nibbling on leftovers from the Christmas feast.

"How did you know to come, Your Grace, at this hour and in this weather?"

Václav turned a log with an iron rod. "You were missing from our Christmas celebration, and God directed our steps."

We bade the family goodnight and began our return to the castle. Though the uphill trek was more difficult, we had left our burdens behind, and even my heart felt lighter. We reached the summit of the castle hill just as the approaching dawn heralded Saint Stephen's Day. When the sunlight touched my face, I felt reborn.

Chapter 25

*T*HE FEAST OF Epiphany finally arrived. I found no other opportunities to spy on Dragomíra, and Boleslav was confined to his room until the wedding. Despite my anxiety throughout the preparations for the wedding and the feast, the ceremony went smoothly. I helped Václav into his new jewel-encrusted tunic, which was uncomfortably heavy, but he never complained. Ana was breathtaking in her shimmering gown, her unbound hair a rippling cloak of honey beneath the sheer veil. I honestly felt nothing but joy in my heart.

They knelt at the altar rail in the Basilica of St. George, the place where Václav had first noticed her. Father Pavel joined their clasped hands with his long stole to symbolize their holy union. I felt proud of the newlyweds, as if I were their brother, instead of just a servant.

During the ceremony, both Dragomíra and Boleslav remained silent, hiding their usual scowls of disapproval. I wished it meant they had finally come to accept Václav, but I knew they had not. At the wedding feast, however, Boleslav was strangely charming. He humbled himself before his brother and asked forgiveness of his new sister-in-law for his boorish behavior.

Žito and I exchanged glances. What was he up to?

Václav, of course, seemed not to suspect that Boleslav's behavior might just be an act. He placed his brother at his right hand while Přibislava sat on the other side of Ana, happily sharing the evening with the friend who was now a sister. I watched Boleslav whenever I had a free moment, but saw no lapse of his forced goodwill. He even managed to stay sober. Dragomíra smiled occasionally, saying a few gracious words to her eldest son and her new daughter-in-law. What was going on? I had to find out.

When the wedding party finally escorted the bride and groom to the bridal chamber in Václav's tower, I saw Dragomíra and Boleslav leave the hall, followed by Ladislav and a handful of lesser *voyvodes*. Using the cover of retiring banquet guests, I noted that the conspirators' destination was Dragomíra's old rooms. I made my way outside to the vines beneath her window. Making sure no one was watching, although I could hear voices all around, I climbed up and perched on the ledge behind a tree branch, hidden from below as well as from inside the room. I shivered from the cold.

A door opened and light shone from within the room. Low voices murmured until they settled close to the window. I imagined them seated around the table there.

"Well, how did I do?" asked Boleslav.

"An excellent performance, my dear," Dragomíra said. "I am certain that Václav believes your repentance is sincere."

I knew it! I knew Boleslav was false!

"Must I really appear to convert to his religion?" Boleslav asked, his voice petulant now.

Ladislav joined the discussion. "It is the only way to convince the duke so thoroughly that you are admitted to his confidences and councils."

Boleslav snorted. "Since when has the practice of this weakling's religion been a prerequisite to power?"

"Since Duke Václav has made it so," snapped Ladislav. "Do you want the Bohemian crown or no?"

"Of course I do. I've had enough of this soft-bellied excuse for a duke, loving his enemies and debasing himself with peasants."

"And submitting to Saxony," Ladislav added.

"Yes, that too," Boleslav agreed. "But what can I do about his popularity with the Čechs?"

"Make the peasants love you, too," said Dragomíra.

Someone, probably Boleslav, slammed the table with a fist. "I don't want them to love me, Mother. I want their fear and their obedience."

"Until you can take the crown from him, you will have to play along with his religion," said Ladislav. "I see no other way to get under his guard."

The others murmured their agreement. Since they moved away from the window, I could no longer hear what they were plotting. I climbed down without first scanning my surroundings, intent on finding Žito.

As soon as my feet touched the ground, a heavy hand pushed me down. I fell forward, and the assailant grabbed my hair and yanked back my head, exposing my throat. When I heard a knife pulled out of its sheath, I remembered my own dagger and fumbled for it.

Before I could act, the man jerked, and a moan escaped his lips. He let go of me and fell to the ground. I spun around and saw Žito holding his own blood-stained knife.

"Haven't I told you to watch your back?" he whispered, frowning.

I swallowed and glanced down at the dead man. His blood made a dark spot on the snow. "Who was it?" I asked.

Žito put a finger to his lips and pointed up at Dragomíra's window. "One of the guards," he whispered, "still loyal to her." He wiped off his blade, sheathed the dagger, and picked up the body. "Cover the blood," he said before he strode away.

I kicked snow over it and hurried to follow him.

When we finally had the chance to talk to Václav, we could not convince our master that the danger from Boleslav and others was real. As Žito later put it, Duke Václav's head was firmly in the clouds of his idealism. Partly because of his newly married joy and partly because of his desire to believe the best of everyone, Václav trusted that Boleslav had sincerely repented of his evil.

"What can we do, if he won't believe us?" I asked Žito. Then I remembered with clarity how Václav had not believed my warning about the danger to his grandmother all those years ago, either. My heart was heavy with worry. How could my master be so blind to his brother's motives when he could see everything else so clearly?

Žito's gaze met my own. "We will be vigilant," he said, "and pray that we can keep him from becoming the victim of his own kindness."

Chapter 26

FOR MANY MONTHS life at the castle fell into the peaceful rhythm of the seasons. Though he was no longer a prisoner there, Boleslav spent most of his time at his own castle. I felt unnerved by the fact that he now had free rein to invent all manner of evil against Václav. Dragomíra, as far as we knew, lived most of the year at her old home in the country north of Bohemia. But in my uncertainty, I often imagined late night sessions between my former mistress, her son, and their conspirators. Whenever I left Praha to accompany Václav on any journey, I found myself spending the entire time listening for sounds of ambush. Concern for my master's safety dominated all my thoughts. I never forgot what I had heard on that cold Epiphany night.

Almost two years to the day after their wedding, Václav announced at dinner one night that Ana was expecting a child. The new Přemyslid heir would be born sometime in May. Boleslav, the current heir, looked startled. For a moment I saw a flash of his true feelings, but he quickly masked them with a forced smile and stood to make a toast.

"May God grant you and the little one health and long life, dear sister," he said to Ana. She lowered her gaze, blushing. I had never seen her look so radiant.

Boleslav excused himself shortly thereafter. To this day, I regret not following him.

It was mid-May, on a sunny day when the fields and gardens burst with color and life. Žito and I waited with Václav while Přibislava and the midwives assisted Ana to deliver her child. My master flinched every time he heard Ana cry out. Helpless tears filled his eyes, as he spent those eternal hours in prayer.

It was dark when at last Přibislava came to the door, her face ashen.

"Is she?" Václav began.

Přibislava shuddered. "She will live, Brother. But the baby did not survive."

Václav swallowed. "When may I see her?"

Přibislava grasped his hand and kissed him. "She sleeps now, but come in and be ready when she wakes." She wiped away the tears on my master's cheeks. "She will need the comfort of your presence then."

Václav nodded, and it tore my heart to see the terrible grief on his face. He turned to Žito. "Will you stand here and guard the door from intrusion?"

Žito bowed. "Yes, my lord."

"And Poidevin, will you come and pray with me 'til Ana wakes?"

I went down on one knee and pressed his free hand to my forehead.

We entered quietly, Václav still holding his sister's hand. The two midwives were cleaning up. A pile of bloody rags lay on the floor. In a basket rested something small wrapped in a cloth. Přibislava noticed Václav staring at it.

"Yes, Brother, that is your son."

He went to the basket and gently picked up the bundle, turning back the cloth to reveal an infant's still, peaceful face. Bowing his head over the body, Václav stumbled to the adjoining chapel and knelt at the altar, his heart broken. I knelt beside him, supporting him in the only way I knew how.

After a long time, at least an hour, my master arose and tenderly covered the baby's face. He placed the body in the basket and turned to his wife. She lay in their big canopied bed, her face white, and her long hair tangled and dull. Václav, at least, had seemed to find peace and strength in that hour, for when Ana opened her eyes, he was ready to comfort her. I slipped out the door to stand guard with Žito.

It took several months before Ana fully recovered both in body and spirit. Václav threw himself into the care and governing of his people, so I felt compelled to spend more time with her and Přibislava, trying to stir them from their grief.

One day when Ana had fallen asleep, Přibislava walked with me to the door.

"I wish I could take away her sorrow," I said. "But perhaps my presence hinders her recovery, making her think about my master when he must be away."

"No, Poidevin," she said, placing her small hand on my arm. "Ana loves you and finds great comfort in your presence. I only wish my brother could spare more time for her, though I know he has a kingdom to rule." Přibislava glanced at her sleeping sister-in-law before turning back and gripping my hand. "That is why your visits are so important to her now. Ana values your kindness and loyalty both to her and to Václav."

I stared at her, dumbstruck. Would I ever get used to the idea that I, an insignificant servant, could matter to people I loved?

Then Přibislava surprised me even more. Smiling at my reaction, she stood on tiptoe and kissed my cheek. My hand automatically touched the place, and I turned to leave while my feet still touched the ground.

Chapter 27

COLOR RETURNED TO Ana's cheeks as the leaves on the trees blushed with autumn hues. As the weather grew colder, Václav began to stay in Praha. His presence seemed to help Ana more than anything else did.

One evening between Christmas and Epiphany, Václav, Ana, Přibislava, Žito, and I had dinner in the duke's room. I helped a servant bring up the food, and after he returned to the kitchen, I poured the wine. Of all the state and private dinners I had ever attended, this one was the best, not because of the food. I was in the company of the four people I loved most. In their presence I could forget the cares of the world. I was so relaxed and in such high spirits that I grabbed a bowl of apples on the table and passed one to each.

"What is this, Poidevin?" Ana asked.

"A custom I remembered from my earliest days, my lady." I picked up a knife from the table. "We are supposed to cut the apple to reveal the seeds. If yours are in the shape of a star, you will have good luck."

Václav raised his brows, but he did not chide me. Had I erred again? Perhaps this was a custom from the old religion. Each of us cut our apple.

"Look, Poidevin," said Přibislava, holding up her apple half. "A star."

I smiled at her, though inwardly I felt sick with dread. Inside my apple there was no star.

"My seeds form the cross," my master said. "A cross seems a much more fitting shape than a star for us as Christians."

"Mine are the same as yours," Ana said, showing him her apple.

"And mine," said Žito. He glanced at me as if he were trying to remember something.

I didn't have the heart to tell them what the shape of the cross meant according to the old superstition.

The long winter drew to a close, and as spring approached, Václav quietly announced that Ana was expecting another child late in the summer. A cautious excitement grew in the castle. To keep his anxiety under control, my master devoted himself to overseeing the last stages of construction on the rotunda, the round stone church he had planned to honor Saint Vitus.

"Who is Saint Vitus?" I asked. "You have never told me."

"Saint Vitus," he explained as we watched the Germanic stone masons at work, "was a young man who lived on a far away island called Sicily. At an early age he showed great faith in God, and while still very young, he cast out an evil spirit from the son of the Roman emperor. The Romans pagans at the time accused Vitus of sorcery and had him executed."

In my imagination the parallels were clear. The pagan emperor was Boleslav, and my master was the pious saint. Suddenly remembering the crosses we had found in our apples, I wondered if this holy place dedicated to a young martyr would someday become Václav's final resting place.

The rotunda was dedicated on Saint Vitus' feast, just five days before the summer solstice. The bishop of Ratisbon came for the ceremony, and afterward in the great hall I overheard murmurings against the Germanic bishop as well as the masons who had built the church. There were extra grumblings anyway at this time of year, because the annual tribute to Henry the Fowler had to be collected and paid. Perhaps my master should have moved the dedication to another time, so the people would have time to calm their anger.

When I mentioned this to Žito, he snorted.

"Do you forget our master's heart?" He crossed his arms. "We could not have swayed him to hold the ceremony at any time other than the saint's actual feast day."

As it was, the day following the dedication, Václav asked for me immediately after his morning meal with the peasant petitioners.

"Poidevin." He looked me over from head to toe.

"Yes, my lord?" I felt self-conscious under his scrutiny.

"I want you to accompany me to the court of Henry the Fowler this year."

"In Saxony?" My old fears whispered tales of monsters in that foreign land, but reason returned when I reminded myself there were no such creatures as vampires or werewolves. The priests of the old religion used fear to keep ignorant peasants under their control. My master had taught me to have faith in God and let go of pagan ideas. Even though I was anxious about the long journey into the unknown, I wanted to be at Václav's side.

"Twenty men-at-arms will accompany us," Václav continued, "for we will be taking the Fowler's tribute with us."

My eyes widened. "And Žito?"

"He will remain here to watch over Ana." Václav beckoned me closer and inspected my tunic. "You will need a new set of clothes, however, before you can appear at King Henry's court."

"New clothes, my lord?" I knew that I had long outgrown my green tunic, but Bora had sewn a wide piece of cloth to the hem in order to keep it an acceptable length. She'd also patched my stockings more times than I could remember.

He stood and gathered up his formal robe. "I shall give them to you tonight. We leave in the morning."

⁂

When I told Žito of my dubious good fortune, he already knew.

"The way will be long and treacherous," he said. "I don't think twenty guards are enough, but our master disagrees. You should consider yourself the twenty-first," he said, charging me to guard the duke with my life if necessary.

Since I'd grown to manhood, Žito and I regularly practiced hand-to-hand combat with daggers. I'd finally learned the art of disarming my opponent.

"Be sure to use your head, Poidevin," were his parting words that evening. "And never forget to watch your back."

⁂

In Václav's tower that night, my master presented me with an embroidered linen tunic, new stockings, cross-garters, and soft leather shoes. Afraid to soil the fine red fabric, I could only stare at the garments.

"Take them, Poidevin," he said. "They're yours."

"Try them on," Ana said, lowering herself into a chair.

"Yes," added Přibislava. "I want to see how you are going to look at the Fowler's court."

So I, a lowly servant, slipped into the adjoining room and put on the first and only finery I have ever worn. I felt like a different person in those clothes, and it must have shown when I stepped back into the room for inspection.

"What a handsome figure you cut, Poidevin!" said Ana.

"Let me trim your hair, and you could almost pass for a *voyvode*." Přibislava got her shears and told me sit on a low stool. I hadn't realized how shaggy my hair had become since the winter. Hanks of it lay on the floor, yet what remained was still shoulder-length.

"There," Přibislava said, satisfied. "You will make my brother proud."

Václav clapped my shoulder. "You have always made me proud, Poidevin, no matter what you were wearing."

With a bow and stammered thanks, I fled before my discomfort got the best of me and I said something utterly stupid.

Chapter 28

OUR PARTY LEFT the following morning. The stable master gave me the sturdy, calm mare I preferred to ride whenever I accompanied my master. We had several pack animals as well, to carry the Fowler's tribute of silver pieces as well as supplies for the journey.

For the first several days, still within Bohemia's borders, I felt uneasy only at night. My master and I did not have our usual discussions because after our evening prayers he continued to pray for Ana and the safe birth of their child. Since I was the duke's personal servant, I wasn't included in the watch rotation. Instead, I spent much of each night sitting near my master while he prayed. I tried to pray too, but old fears of evil in the forest crowded my thoughts, and I found myself wishing I could remain close to the campfires to shut out the terror I could not seem to banish.

The night before we crossed into Saxony, Václav ended his prayers earlier than usual and turned to face me.

"Tomorrow we will leave Bohemia," he said quietly. "I have made this journey before, but since you have not, I want to reassure you that there is nothing to be afraid of."

I lowered my eyes, ashamed that he had seen the lingering fear there. "Thank you, my lord. I confess I have been anxious about what we would see in Saxony."

"The land is much like ours. There are rivers and forests, villages and farms. The people are also like ours: some are friendly and some are not. Many are Christians, but there are a few who still follow their old pagan religion." He paused and I glanced up. Václav stared into the nearest campfire, but his gaze was far away.

I thought to ask if the pagan religion of Saxony was anything like that in Bohemia, but realized it didn't matter. Not long ago my first impulse would have been to find out what the foreign spirits of rivers and ponds desired for a sacrifice in order to allow travelers to cross or drink from their waters. Now that I knew those spirits were not real, I had only to find a way to muster the courage I needed as my master did.

The weather was kind to us the first several days in Saxony, except that it grew hot by midday. Václav urged us to keep moving, even in the heat. Though no one knew the reason for his urgency, he confided to me that the Fowler had commanded him to attend an important meeting of the German king's subject dukes. Of course, he wanted to hurry back to Ana as soon as the gathering was over.

At midday I could forget about the hidden things in the strange forests and mountains and rivers all around us. But as twilight fell at the end of each day, the mists would rise and unfamiliar cries sounded in the dark. It was hard to concentrate on prayers or even sleep, no matter how exhausted I was.

Václav remained an anchor of calm as we traveled through the alien Saxon land. Five of his twenty guards were chosen because they spoke the German tongue fluently. Whenever we came upon a farm or town, these men were sent with silver coins to purchase the supplies we needed.

At last we reached a mighty river, one greater than the Vltava that flowed beside our own city of Praha. Across the river, standing atop a formidable cliff, was an imposing stone castle. It made our massive wooden castle seem flimsy and insubstantial. How did the Saxons build such a fortress? Did some of the stone masons whom Václav had hired to build Saint Vitus's rotunda also work on this edifice?

I absently dismounted with the others but scarcely paid attention as we stepped onto the ferry boat. Because I could not take my eyes from the sight of that stone fortress, I missed most of the wide river and its marvels, and hardly noticed my horse's unsteady footing until we walked off the ferry and onto dry land.

A walled town lay at the foot of the cliff. The castle loomed above us. I remounted and followed my master while our party entered the town.

"Do we have the time, Your Grace?" the head guard asked the duke when Václav spoke to him.

"There is time," my master assured him. "Come, Poidevin. I will pray at the church while you change into your finery."

The two of us approached another magnificent stone structure. The guards held our horses while Václav went into the church. I grabbed the saddlebag containing my new clothes and found a place to dress nearby. I waited with the guards for Václav as the sun moved higher in the sky. At last he came out of the church.

"Is it noon yet?" he asked.

The guard captain squinted at the sun. "Just past, I would say, Your Grace."

Václav silently mounted and led us up the winding road to the top of the cliff. When we reached the gatehouse, he spoke to the helmeted guards in German. One pointed to our party and shook his head, but my master spoke again. At last the guard held up two fingers.

The duke spoke to the guard captain again. "The men are to remain here. Only Poidevin and I are allowed inside, with the tribute, of course."

The guard saluted. "Yes, Your Grace, I understand him." He leaned toward my master and spoke quietly, "Be careful, my lord. I sense hostility here."

Václav inclined his head. "Come, Poidevin."

I followed him, even though the open maw of the gate made me think of a hungry lion's mouth.

Chapter 29

WHILE WE RODE through the stone gatehouse, I felt the stares of the guards upon us. One soldier gripped the shaft of his lance, daring us to give him an excuse to use it. My master did not seem bothered at all.

Though my heart pounded, I tried to imitate Duke Václav's calm assurance, at least outwardly. I remembered how Daniel's three friends answered when they refused to worship the king's idol and were thrown in the fiery furnace. I had gasped aloud the first time my master read that story to me, but he laughed and reminded me that the story wasn't finished. Daniel's friends were saved because of their faith that day. I hoped we would be, too.

Just inside the gatehouse we were met by a score of guards who blocked our further passage with their spears. Did they really think the two of us were a threat?

"Your Grace," said one of the soldiers in our own Slavic tongue, "you must dismount and leave your horses here. We shall escort you to the king's council chambers."

My master would not have taken offense even if the man had shown him no respect. "We are in your debt, soldier," he said as he handed over the reins.

The man who took my horse's reins could not help but notice how my hands trembled.

We followed the two guards up the stairs and down a long corridor. I glanced over at Václav, and he winked at me.

"Remember Daniel," he said, "God will protect us from the jaws of the lion."

"Yes, my lord," I said with a tight smile. The fact that his thoughts echoed mine gave me courage.

When we reached Henry the Fowler's council room, another pair of guards stood by. They opened the carved wooden doors at our approach.

The first thing I saw in the room was the long trestle table with King Henry, wearing a red mantle and his crown of state, seated at the far end. Many other lords sat around the table. They all stared at my master with what could only be distaste and disapproval.

Václav seemed to see no one but the Fowler. He strode toward him, and I kept up with his long strides. When he went down on one knee at King Henry's side, I knelt behind him, not daring to lift my eyes above the level of Václav's boot sole.

"I beg your pardon, Your Highness," Václav said in a clear voice. "My wife will give birth to my heir soon, and I lost track of the hour while I prayed in your church below that God's mercy be upon her and the baby." This he spoke in Latin and, apparently, repeated in German for the benefit of those present who only understood that guttural tongue.

I glanced up to catch a glimpse of the king's face. He was the same regal-looking man whom I'd seen several years ago, first with his invading army, and then at our humble wooden castle. His frown of displeasure melted at my master's words, and he indicated that Václav should rise. The king began speaking to my master in German, so I did not understand the rest of the meeting. After the Fowler seated Duke Václav beside him, I stood, like the others around the table, behind his carved wooden chair.

The meeting lasted until evening. I was grateful to my duke for outfitting me so handsomely. Indeed, had I worn my other clothes, I would have shamed both him and myself.

Before the king dismissed the meeting, he called upon the Duke of Bohemia, who had the guards bring in the annual tribute. Václav gave a speech I could not understand, but it seemed to greatly please King Henry. It pleased him so much, in fact, that he bestowed upon my master the kiss of peace as well as one of his several rings. The Fowler gave his own animated speech, which I noticed was greeted with little enthusiasm by his subject dukes. They put on a show of goodwill for the King's benefit, but I had learned by watching Boleslav and Dragomíra how to tell when someone's outward behavior was false. Of course, it wasn't my master's fault if men and women harbored envy toward him. He did nothing out of selfish motives. I wondered, though, if Václav was unaware of their smoldering resentment. If he did notice it, he must have chosen to ignore it. Perhaps that was part of the reason he inspired such devotion in both the lowliest of peasants and the great king of the Saxons.

After the banquet that evening, we were shown to our room. We climbed a spiral staircase made of stone to the top of one of the castle's towers. As soon as we were alone, I turned to my master.

"My lord, what did King Henry give you at the end of the meeting?" I tried to see the ring on his finger.

He pulled it off and handed it to me. The ring was gold set with black stones. On its face was the imperial eagle. "The Fowler made me a king today, Poidevin."

"A king? King of Bohemia?" When he nodded, I leaped into the air. "Then, my lord, no one can complain anymore! You are equal with King Henry—"

Václav stopped me with a gesture. "No, Poidevin. I may be a king in name, but Bohemia must still pay tribute to Saxony." I gave him back the ring, and he continued. "The Fowler wished only to honor me before his nobles. The title means nothing, really."

I didn't agree, but I respected my master too much to argue with him. If only Boleslav had been here to see how King Henry loved Václav!

I know my master wanted to return home quickly, but on the following day the Fowler requested his presence on a stag hunt. I went, too, still wearing my finery. Watching how King Henry conducted himself I learned why he had come to be known as "the Fowler." Instead of asking his servants to do so, he personally set and checked several bird snares.

When the party returned to the castle with a stag tied to a pack horse, I realized that the object of this hunt had not been the game or quarry at all, but to solidify alliances. I was grateful to be able to stand at banquet and bear the cup for my master, for I don't believe I could have sat still even if King Henry had commanded it.

The return trip home took only nine days. The men-at-arms were in a festive mood, especially once we crossed into Bohemia. My master continued to pray at each stop, and I found my own thoughts turning more and more to Ana. Had the baby been born yet? If so, had both mother and child survived this time?

As soon as we came in sight of Praha, Václav shielded his eyes to better see whether a banner flew on the rampart of the castle.

He turned to me. "Poidevin, what do you see with your long eyes?"

I squinted and just made out the banner as it unfurled in the wind. "Why, it is not your colors, but a flag of solid violet."

He grinned and threw his arms wide. "Thanks be to our most merciful God!" he cried.

"What? What is it, my lord?" The guards crowded closer, curious now.

Václav smiled at us all. "That banner is Žito's signal. Bohemia has a new Přemysl heir. I have a son!"

We needed no urging to follow our Duke as he kicked his horse to a gallop.

Chapter 30

OY AND CELEBRATION I could never have imagined greeted us when we entered the gates! The entire castle was decorated as if for a grand celebration. The servants wore their best clothes. Bora ran out of her hut to curtsy and hand Duke Václav a bouquet of summer flowers. He politely accepted all the sincere words of congratulations, but I knew he could barely contain his desire to see Ana and the child.

We took the steps two and three at a time in our haste to reach his tower. There, in the big canopy bed, sat a rosy-cheeked Ana nursing a healthy-looking infant. Václav fell to his knees and uttered his thanks before leaping up and planting a kiss on Ana's smiling mouth. Přibislava came to stand beside me, surely feeling as proud as I was in that moment.

"When was he born?" I whispered.

"Just three days ago," she said. "He was so pink and strong, and he cried so heartily, I was sure you could hear him all the way in Saxony!"

Perhaps remembering what had happened to the first child, Václav wanted to have his son baptized as soon as possible. Plans were made to hold the ceremony in the new church. Dragomíra was invited, but sent word that she was ill and could not travel.

Přibislava pulled me aside. "Guess what, Poidevin? Václav and Ana want me to be the baby's godmother."

"If there is a godmother," I said, teasing her, "does that mean there has to be a godfather, too?"

She nodded, and her face grew solemn. "I wish it could be you, Poidevin, but my brother has asked Boleslav."

"Boleslav?" I held my tongue before Přibislava. After all, Boleslav was her brother, too. Perhaps she, like Václav, wanted to believe Boleslav's conversion was sincere. Was I overly suspicious? I didn't think so. I could, however, allow for the possibility that the graces of the font might change Boleslav for my master's sake.

A week later, I wore my finery for the last time. I entered the round stone church of Saint Vitus, feeling almost as if I were part of Václav's family. As I listened to the Latin words of Father Pavel's prayers, peace covered me like a mantle. I watched Václav and Ana share the joy of their infant son. Beside me, Přibislava wiped away happy tears with the back of her hand. Boleslav, however, stood silently at his brother's right hand. The candle-light threw harsh shadows on his face, shadows that revealed his smoldering evil thoughts. It was plain to me, if to no one else, that Boleslav resented his new nephew, for now his dreams of usurping the crown of Bohemia had been foiled by the birth of the infant Přemysl heir.

If only Václav had seen that look! But his gaze was focused on his son and on the words of the ritual. When the time came to name the baby, my master spoke reverently: "His name is Přemysl Zbraslav, Prince of the Čechs."

With those words, Boleslav's jaw momentarily tightened, and then he smiled at Václav. The transition was so fast that I briefly doubted what I'd seen.

That evening a feast was held in honor of the baby prince. Boleslav ate and drank and outwardly celebrated with his brother. Still, I could see a plan brewing behind his dark eyes. Václav may well have laughed had I told him. But the evil was there, all the same.

⚜

Less than a month later, just after the beginning of autumn, Václav received a message from Boleslav.

"He is dedicating a new church at his castle and wishes me to come." Václav smacked the parchment against his palm. "I told you he would come around! He has finally seen that the ways of God are true, and far better than the darkness of pagan ritual and superstition."

Žito and I exchanged worried looks. "When shall we leave?" Žito asked.

Václav searched each of our faces. "I shall leave in the morning, and only Poidevin will go with me."

Žito took a step forward. "No, my lord! You cannot go there without an armed escort. It could be a trap!"

Václav laid a hand on Žito's shoulder. "My faithful friend, I must allow Boleslav the opportunity to demonstrate his new faith. Arriving with an armed escort would be an insult."

I protested. Ana and Přibislava also voiced their unease.

My master held up both hands, silencing us all. "Your concern is appreciated but not necessary. God will watch over me and Poidevin."

With a sigh, I slumped against Přibislava's chair. She gripped my hand, and I once again found the strength to stand on my own. Long ago I had thought of myself as her protector. Now I realized Přibislava had so much strength of faith and character, she did not need a guard. I knelt and kissed her hand with all the devotion I had for her, for I feared I might never return to see her face again.

Chapter 31

VÁCLAV AND I said our goodbyes before we left for Boleslav's castle. I noticed every detail of the bright autumn day. Ana stood on the castle steps holding a squirming infant, her eyes full of love for both her child and her husband. When Přibislava kissed Václav's cheek, she lifted a trembling hand in farewell, and her eyes meeting mine shone with tears. Žito's brows thundered together as he studied our master for signs that he had changed his mind and would allow him and a score of armed men to accompany us. It was so hard to turn from them and ride away.

After we passed through the castle gates, we met Bora on her way to the well.

"God be with you, Your Grace." She set down her bucket and curtsied. "And, Poidevin," she added, "visit an old woman when you return."

"I will, Bora." I forced a smile, for her sake.

While riding through the city of Praha on our way to the river, people ran to greet their beloved duke. He called most of them by name and asked how this one's sick child was doing, or if that one had found his lost sheep. I realized why it did not matter to Václav that Henry the Fowler had given him the title of king. To my master, it was more important to love his people than to rule over them.

We reached Boleslav's castle that afternoon. He, of course, played the cordial host to his brother, showing him the small stone church he had built. I noticed that the wooden door had a brass lion's head with the ring of the handle in its mouth. Another lion's mouth, I thought grimly. How appropriate where Boleslav was concerned.

The feast in Václav's honor that night became loud and unruly with the shouts and laughter of drunken men drowning out the raucous music. It made such a contrast to the feasts held at Václav's castle. While I hovered behind my master, I listened to the men's boastful talk and watched their reddened eyes measure the duke. I saw both sides of Boleslav, whereas my master seemed to see only one. The outward Boleslav deferred to his brother, the duke, but the inward one seethed with resentment. In this one thing only Václav was blind. He had always seen his brother the way he wished and hoped he would be, and not as he truly was.

It would be nearly impossible for me to protect my master from Boleslav. Is that what God expected of me—or was all this part of some greater plan I could not yet understand?

Before we retired for the night, Václav stood to offer a toast. Boleslav, I am sure, thought that his brother would take the opportunity to flatter him. Instead, my master honored the one whose feast was coming two days later.

"Let us drink to the Archangel Michael," Václav said, lifting his cup. "May he fight the Evil One on our behalf and usher our souls safely into the peace and joy of life everlasting."

No one spoke while he drained his cup. The drunken faces stared at him in confusion, and Boleslav's face puffed up like a toad's. I couldn't stand the tension, so I shouted, "Amen!"

The noise resumed as we left the hall, following a servant to our quarters.

As soon as the door closed behind us, I turned to Václav in distress.

"My lord, we must leave tonight! Can't you see that Boleslav plans to harm you?" I hated myself for being so angry with him.

Václav gripped my shoulders. "Poidevin, I am not blind. I know my brother; I know that he has listened to the counsel of wicked men. Yet I have also seen glimpses of conscience and remorse in him since Father Pavel baptized him."

My voice shook with barely controlled fury. "But why did you knowingly endanger yourself to come here?"

Václav's face grew sorrowful. "Because," he said quietly, "I have placed myself in God's hands for Boleslav's sake." His face expressed a mixture of both sadness and love. "If by coming here in good faith I can save my brother's soul, then there will be rejoicing in heaven. But even if the worst happens, I will place my trust in God. Isn't that what our faith is all about, Poidevin?"

I shrugged off Václav's explanation. How could a man as wise and farseeing as my master choose to make himself so vulnerable? Václav had such a good heart, but it seemed as if his own goodness made him incapable of imagining the evil Boleslav plotted against him. I was afraid to consider just how much it would cost my master to love this brother who despised him.

Almost as if he'd read my thoughts, Václav reminded me of an earlier lesson. "Even wicked people love others who love them, Poidevin. But Christ says we are blessed if we love those who hate us. He tells us to love even our enemies."

I looked up at him. "But how, my lord?" My voice sounded angrier than I intended.

He took a deep breath. "Because, faithful Poidevin, in doing so we finally begin to understand how God can love us. At one time or another, each of us is an enemy of God. Loving our enemies is the only way we can hope to become like Christ."

My anger found its focus then, and the question I'd not been able to ask for years poured out unbidden.

"But if God truly loves us, then how can he allow such evil to exist? Why does he let good people suffer?" The last word came out as a sob.

Václav didn't answer right away. He folded his hands and gathered his thoughts, allowing me to calm myself a little.

"Do you remember the story of Adam and Eve and the serpent?" he finally asked.

I nodded but did not speak.

"The serpent was Satan, the source of evil. God permits him to test us, but not more than we can bear with his grace." He paused. "God brings good from evil; he makes use of our suffering to purify our souls, just like the refiner's fire purifies gold. The pain and betrayal we experience bring us closer to Jesus Christ, who suffered and died for us on the cross. God gives us the power to do good even in the face of evil, just as he did. We can do this because we know that whatever we suffer in this life is nothing compared with the joys of heaven awaiting the faithful."

Though my head was spinning, I fell to my knees and covered my face with my hands.

"Forgive me, Master, for my anger and my doubts. I have no right to question you or God."

"There is nothing to forgive," he said, "but I will forgive you because you ask it." He raised me up and stared into my eyes. "Tell me, Poidevin, what is the worst Boleslav can do?"

That was easy. "He could kill you."

"But I am not afraid to die, because I know something far better awaits me."

"Then," I stammered, "then he could kill Ana and little Zbraslav. And if Boleslav became duke he would make things difficult for all the people."

Václav grasped my shoulders and stared into my eyes. "Our lives are as brief as a summer storm, Poidevin. We have so little time here to live and love and serve. I am only God's humble servant; he is the true king of Bohemia, and his purpose will be accomplished, no matter who sits on the throne. The light of truth and faith in Christ will always shine in the darkness, because in the end Jesus Christ will be victorious."

He did not wait for my reply. Instead Václav gestured for me to kneel with him in prayer. I asked God to deliver my master just as he had saved Daniel in the lion's den, and Daniel's three friends from the fiery furnace. But then I remembered that none of them had expected to be saved. Believing they would die, their faith in God never wavered. At last, I prayed to have faith as strong as Daniel's, as strong as that of the men in the fiery furnace—as strong as Václav's.

Chapter 32

I DID NOT SLEEP well that night, but kept dreaming about the Archangel Michael. I saw a resolute look on his face as he wielded a flaming sword of justice. It was hard to imagine that he would help dying souls into the afterlife. From the first time I'd heard of him, he seemed so fierce to me. But perhaps, like Žito, the outward ferocity masked a tender heart.

At first light, Václav and I awoke and dressed for early Mass. I started to put my dagger on my belt, but my master stopped me.

"We should not arm ourselves to enter the house of God," he said quietly. "I will leave my sword here and you must leave your dagger."

I bit back my protest and simply nodded. There was so much I wanted to say to him, but the time for words had passed. We left our rooms and headed down to Boleslav's new stone church.

We approached as the building glowed, awash in the rays of the rising sun. All the hairs on my neck stood on end. But when I glanced around, I saw no one at all. Even this early, I thought, there should be servants about.

I turned back to my master. Václav met my gaze, his face lit with peace and a smile. I was warmed by his continued hope and faith and at the same time troubled.

When we reached the heavy door, it was locked. That, too, was odd. Suddenly, I heard the muffled stamp of feet behind us. I whirled around, my hand reaching for the dagger that was not there.

"Brother," Boleslav said in that sneering voice of his. He was accompanied by a dozen men wearing hooded cloaks to conceal their identities, and perhaps their weapons. My heart pounded in fear for my master.

Václav slowly turned. "We are well met at the house of God," he said, holding out his hands as if to embrace his brother.

In answer Boleslav pulled out a sword from under his cloak and slashed at Václav's unprotected head. My master held up his hands in a warding gesture, and the deflected blade cut his head in a glancing blow that left a gash in his scalp. Strangely, no blood gushed forth.

Boleslav gasped and stepped back. Some of his men paused as they drew swords or daggers.

"He does not bleed!" cried one of the hooded figures.

Václav looked at me then with such sadness that tears filled my eyes. I quickly wiped them away, knowing that his sadness was not for himself, or even for me, but for this wretched brother he *still* loved, even now.

I angrily turned on the nearest man and wrenched his dagger arm. Caught by surprise, he loosened his grip long enough for me to wrestle the blade away and plunge it into his neck. His blood fountained over my hands and arms, and his dying body fell to the ground. I only wished it had been Boleslav.

Strong hands pinned my arms behind my back, and others held my head, forcing me to watch. Václav clung to the brass lion handle of the church door, bleeding from several wounds. Then an enraged Boleslav raised a bloody blade.

"I forgive you, Brother," Václav managed to say, before Boleslav plunged the dagger into his back.

My beloved master slumped to the stones. Two of Boleslav's men laid out his lifeless body. When Václav's face came into view, I saw that his sadness had turned to peace once more.

Tears ran unashamedly down my cheeks. I cried, not just for Václav's cruel death, but because I had allowed my anger to betray his goodness at the end. I found myself praying that my master had not seen how I'd taken my own vengeance and killed one of Boleslav's men.

They dragged me to the bowels of the castle and clapped me in irons. The priest we had seen at the church the day before was allowed to visit me. I confessed the murder I had committed and the weakness of my faith in God. Then I asked for one more thing.

"Could you bring me parchment and a quill and ink, Father?" I requested with a heavy heart.

He raised an eyebrow in surprise. "And what purpose would those items serve to one of your position, my son?"

"Do you know Father Pavel at Praha?" I asked. The desperation in my voice would have been apparent to the dullest of men. The priest nodded. "I must write something down for him. It is urgent, Father."

I could not know how long they would keep me in this dungeon. I had days, perhaps, but more likely hours before they hanged me. If they had wanted me to live, they would have brought food or at least water.

Epilogue

And so the priest smuggled writing tools into the dungeon, and I, my master's servant, have written this account of Duke Václav's life and death.

I hear the executioner coming now, so I will finish quickly. I beg any who read this to tell others the truth about my master, so that Boleslav can never erase the memory of Václav's goodness. If my words here are lost, I am at peace, for writing them has helped me see two things clearly. First, I am not afraid to die. I came to faith in Christ through Václav's patient teaching and confessed that faith at my baptism. Now, entrusting God with my eternal soul, I have hope that I will see Václav again in that better place. And second, I hope to tell him that I can forgive Boleslav now. I still cannot love him, but I have learned to pity him, for he will never know the joy and peace that my master and I will share for all time. Come, Archangel! I am ready!

Afterword

ANY OF VÁCLAV'S loyal subjects fled the country; others met a fate similar to Poidevin's. Žito, Ana, and the infant prince were killed, although Přibislava was allowed to live and remained at Castle Praha. The new duke began his long reign and became known as Boleslav the Cruel.

However, his son, Boleslav II, became a Christian, and his daughter, Dubravka, married the prince of Poland and brought faith in Christ to that country for the first time. Perhaps both were influenced by their goodly Aunt Přibislava's stories of Václav and his faithful servant, Poidevin.

The people of Bohemia never forgot their good Duke Václav. In time he became the patron saint of the Čechs. Even today, a statue of Svaty Václav—known in English as Saint Wenceslaus—stands in the main square of the city of Praha (Prague), capital of the Czech Republic. Dressed for battle, he sits astride a horse, holding a banner—a true warrior like Joshua. But, as Poidevin could attest, Václav also ruled with the spirit of Joseph, a humble spirit of wisdom and charity that illuminated the darkness of his times with the light of God's truth.

Author's Note

IN THE TENTH century, the land that is now part of the Czech Republic in Eastern Europe was a duchy known as Bohemia or Čechy (land of the Čechs). Bohemia's capital has been Praha (Prague) for more than a thousand years. The ruling family from the ninth to the fourteenth century was known as the Přemyslid dynasty, after its founder Přemysl. Legend states Přemysl rose from humble beginnings to become the first prince or duke of the Czech people.

The story of the man most English speakers know as Saint Wenceslaus is full of political intrigue. The period often called the Dark Ages was characterized by a long struggle between old pagan practices and the introduction of Christianity to peoples who arrived in Europe in the ninth century. Václav, Poidevin, Saint Ludmila, Dragomíra, Boleslav, Přibislava, King Henry the Fowler of Saxony, Duke Arnulf of Bavaria, Duke Radslav of Kourím, Father Pavel (Paul), Tunna, and Gommon are all historical people. The names of Václav's wife and son are not mentioned in the records, so they have been given fictional names. Žito, Father Balád, Bora, Žibrid, Ladislav, and Jan are all fictional characters.

Because the events of Václav's life happened eleven hundred years ago, there is little surviving documentation and much has to be pieced together through snippets of fact and legend. Even the year of Václav's martyrdom is in question. Older sources state 929 A.D. but some newer sources claim it must have been 935 A.D. Either way, Václav was in his twenties when he died, still a young man, and I have chosen to use the earlier date to emphasize his youth.

Václav died in an era before the process of canonization was reserved to the pope. His sainthood was pronounced by Bishop Detmar (or his successor Bishop Adalbert) of Prague. By the time of King Otto III (980–1002), the Sacramentary of the Catholic Church listed September 28 as the Feast of Saint Wenceslaus, Martyr. In 1925, September 28 was made a state holiday in the Republic of Czechoslovakia. Václav is the patron of the Czech Republic and of brewers. All Czechs, even those who are not Catholic, revere him.

KATY HUTH JONES grew up in a family where creative juices overflowed and made puddles to splash in. She has published five children's books and more than 100 short stories, poems, and articles in magazines and anthologies. When not writing, Katy plays piccolo and flute in a regional symphony. She lives with her husband, Keith, in the beautiful Texas Hill Country. Their two sons, whom she homeschooled, have flown the nest and live creative lives of their own.

Discussion Questions

1. This story takes place eleven hundred years ago in a small country in Eastern Europe. What details take the reader into that time and place, and how is it different from life today?

2. The structure of this story is a "frame" device. What is the device used, and how does it change the story from a simple narrative?

3. Throughout the book the light of truth in the Christian God is contrasted with the darkness of paganism. How many examples and symbols of this contrast can you find?

4. Besides growing from a twelve-year-old slave into a twenty-year-old man, in what ways does the main character Poidevin change by the end of the story?

5. Poidevin has many fears he must overcome, and it takes him many years. What are his specific fears? How do love and devotion to both God and Václav become a more powerful motivation than fear?

6. Once Poidevin is enslaved and taken to Praha, he discovers "I had been in bondage my entire life without

realizing it." What did he mean? Would this also apply to his spiritual life?

7. Even though Poidevin is enslaved and later becomes a personal servant to Duke Václav, he is taught to be a servant of God by his master. Is everyone a servant to someone else? What about kings?

8. Václav teaches Poidevin truths about God through the stories of God's people in the Old Testament. Which ones are specifically mentioned? Do any of them feature "heroes of faith" to you? Why? Who would you consider a faith hero?

9. Most people know Duke Václav as "Good King Wenceslaus" from the old Christmas carol. Can you find the scene that depicts the story told in the carol? How is it different?

10. How do you think this book would have been different if it had been written from Václav's point of view instead of Poidevin's?

ANOTHER EXCITING STORY OF COURAGE AND FAITH FOR TEENS

LORENZO RUIZ, a faithful Catholic husband and father, is falsely accused of murder. Through a series of dramatic and unforeseen events, he discovers that the will of God for him depends on a difficult choice. Lorenzo was imprisoned, tortured, and ultimately executed for his faith in Christ. *Martyred* is a historical novel based on the true story of the first Filipino saint.

MARTYRED:
The Story of Saint Lorenzo Ruiz

The Story of Saint Lorenzo Ruiz

MARTYRED

Pauline TEEN

TEEN

Pauline

Who: The Daughters of St. Paul

What: Pauline Teen—linking your life to Jesus Christ and his Church

When: 24/7

Where: All over the world and on www.pauline.org

Why: Because our life-long passion is to witness to God's amazing love for all people!

How: Inspiring lives of holiness through: Apps, digital media, concerts, websites, social media, videos, blogs, books, music albums, radio, media literacy, DVDs, ebooks, stores, conferences, bookfairs, parish exhibits, personal contact, illustration, vocation talks, photography, writing, editing, graphic
marketing

BOOKS & MEDIA

The Daughters of St. Paul operate book and media centers at the following addresses. Visit, call, or write the one nearest you today, or find us at www.pauline.org.

CALIFORNIA
3908 Sepulveda Blvd, Culver City, CA 90230   310-397-8676
935 Brewster Avenue, Redwood City, CA 94063   650-369-4230
5945 Balboa Avenue, San Diego, CA 92111   858-565-9181

FLORIDA
145 SW 107th Avenue, Miami, FL 33174   305-559-6715

HAWAII
1143 Bishop Street, Honolulu, HI 96813   808-521-2731

ILLINOIS
172 North Michigan Avenue, Chicago, IL 60601   312-346-4228

LOUISIANA
4403 Veterans Memorial Blvd, Metairie, LA 70006 504-887-7631

MASSACHUSETTS
885 Providence Hwy, Dedham, MA 02026   781-326-5385

MISSOURI
9804 Watson Road, St. Louis, MO 63126   314-965-3512

NEW YORK
64 West 38th Street, New York, NY 10018   212-754-1110

SOUTH CAROLINA
243 King Street, Charleston, SC 29401   843-577-0175

TEXAS
Currently no book center; for parish exhibits or outreach evangelization, contact: 210-569-0500 or SanAntonio@ paulinemedia.com or P.O. Box 761416, San Antonio, TX 78245

VIRGINIA
1025 King Street, Alexandria, VA 22314   703-549-3806

CANADA
3022 Dufferin Street, Toronto, ON M6B 3T5   416-781-9131

SMILE God Loves you